STONE ARCH BOOKS
a capstone imprint

STONE ARCH BOOKS™

Published in 2013
A Capstone Imprint
1710 Roe Crest Drive
North Mankato, MN 56003
www.capstonepub.com

Originally published by DC Comics in the U.S. in single magazine form as Superman Adventures #5.

DC Comics
1700 Broadway, New York, NY 10019
A Warner Bros. Entertainment Company

Printed in China by Nordica.
1012/CA21201277
092012 006935NORDS13

Cataloging-in-Publication Data is available at the Library of Congress website:
ISBN: 978-1-4342-4710-0 (library binding)

Summary: The electrically-charged Legion of Superheroes' villainess Livewire surges ahead with a new cause - the complete and utter downfall of all men! Only the Man of Steel has a chance of stopping her, provided she doesn't send a permanent shock to his system first!

STONE ARCH BOOKS

Ashley C. Andersen Zantop *Publisher*
Michael Dahl *Editorial Director*
Donald Lemke & Sean Tulien *Editors*
Heather Kindseth *Creative Director*
Bob Lentz *Designer*
Kathy McColley *Production Specialist*

DC COMICS

Mike McAvennie *Original U.S. Editor*
Rick Burchett & Terry Austin *Cover Artists*

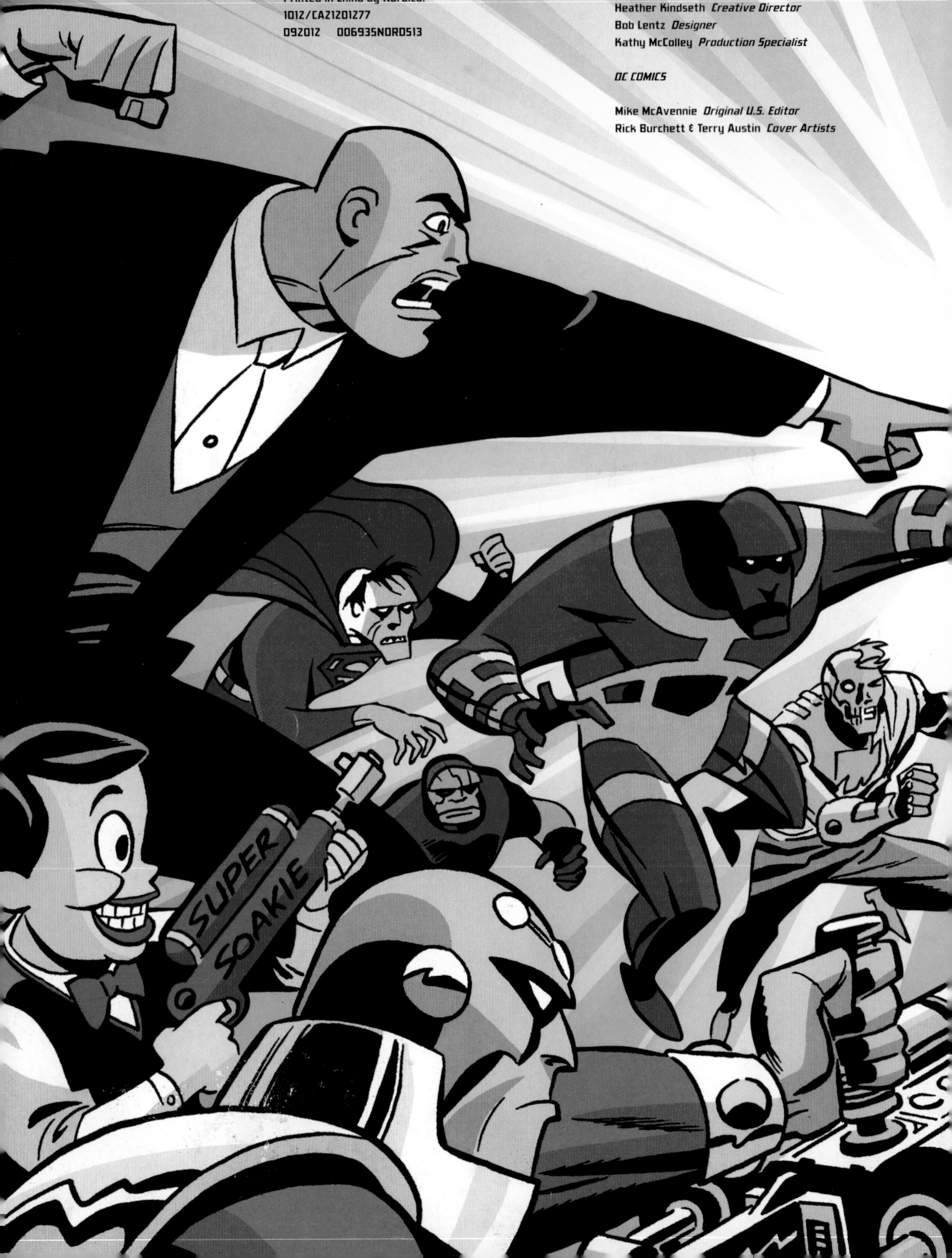
SUPER SOAKIE

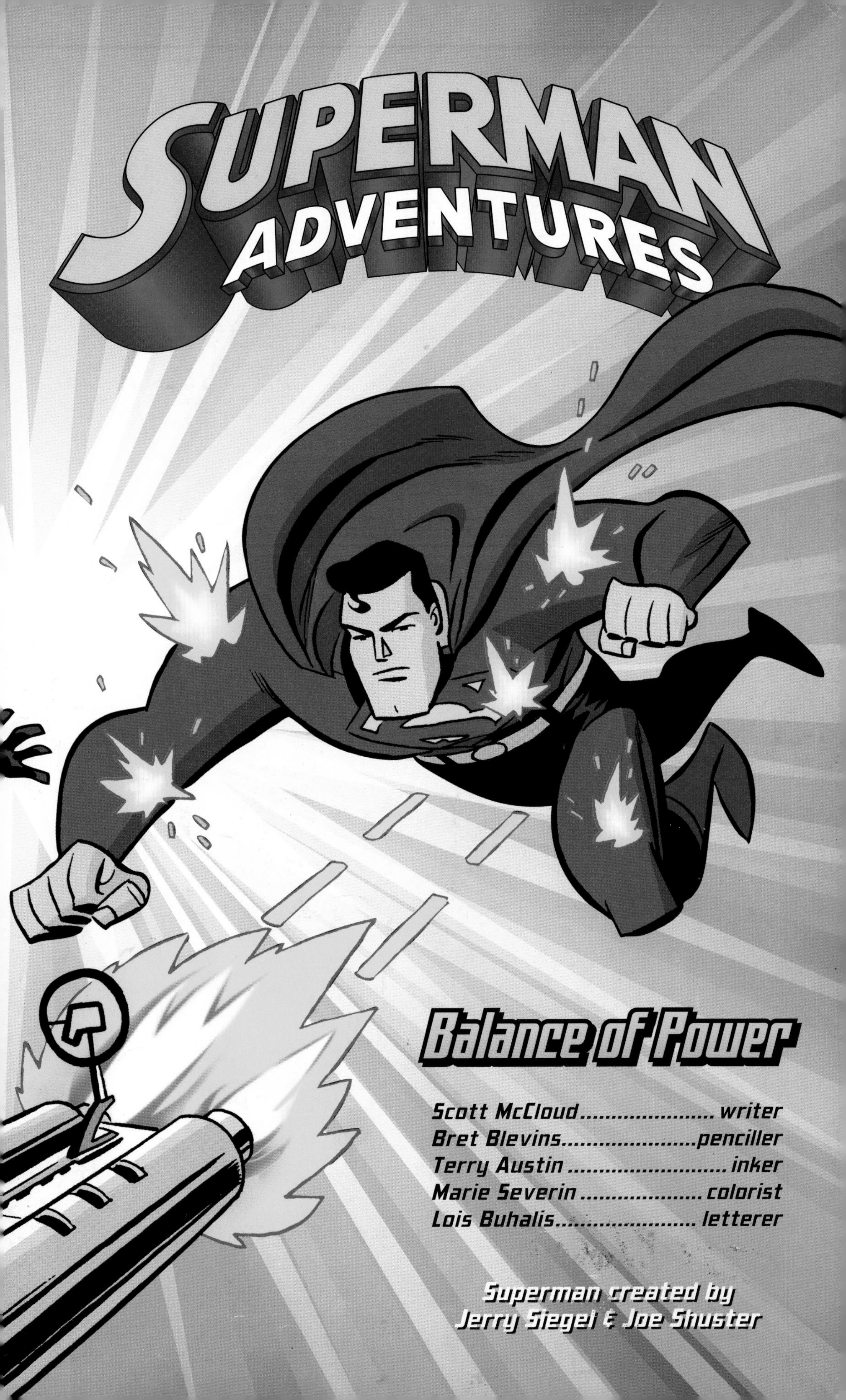
SUPERMAN ADVENTURES
Balance of Power
Scott McCloud........................ writer
Bret Blevins........................penciller
Terry Austin .... inker
Marie Severin .... colorist
Lois Buhalis........................ letterer
Superman created by
Jerry Siegel & Joe Shuster

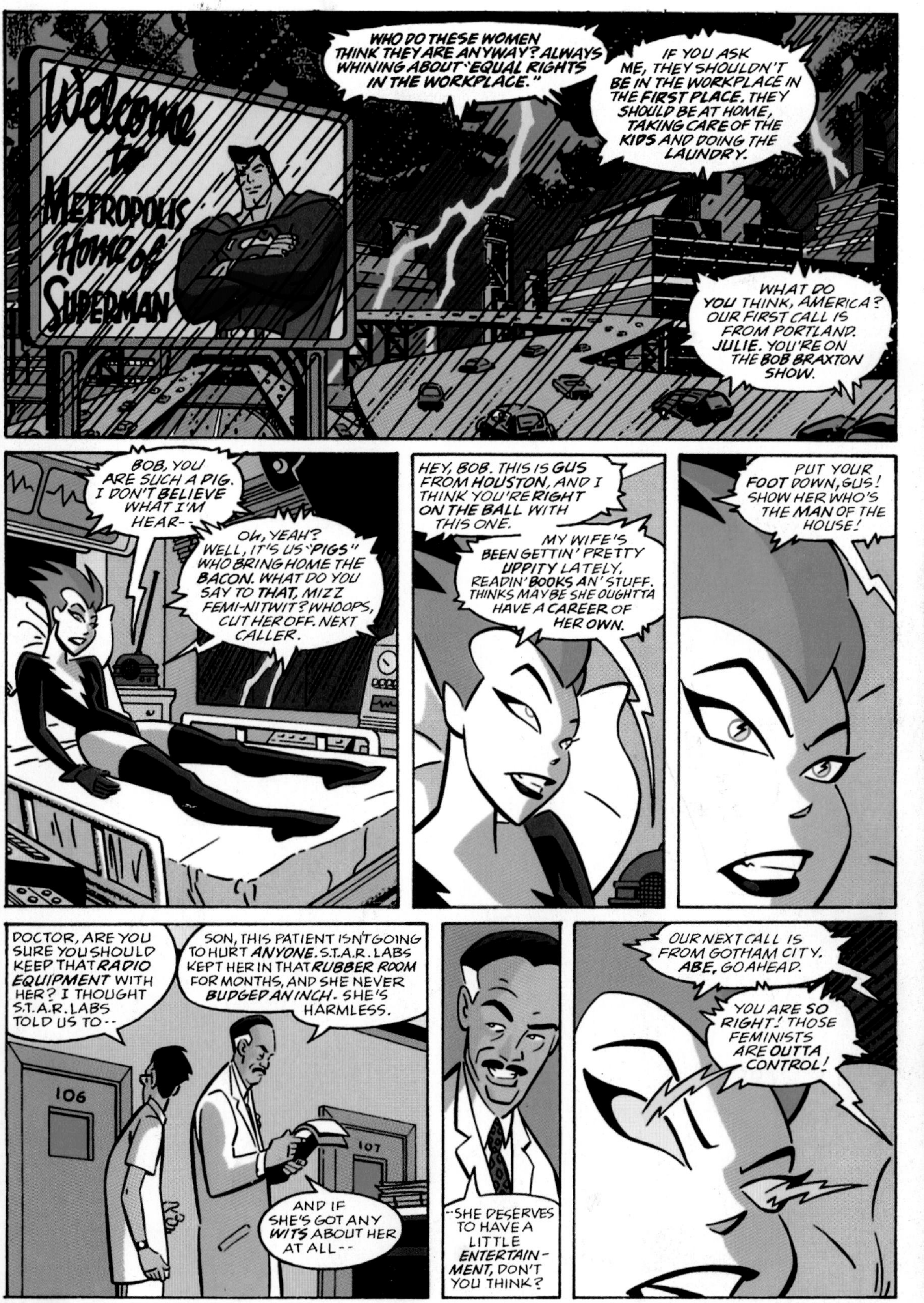
Welcome to Metropolis Home of Superman
WHO DO THESE WOMEN THINK THEY ARE ANYWAY? ALWAYS WHINING ABOUT "EQUAL RIGHTS IN THE WORKPLACE."
IF YOU ASK ME, THEY SHOULDN'T BE IN THE WORKPLACE IN THE FIRST PLACE. THEY SHOULD BE AT HOME, TAKING CARE OF THE KIDS AND DOING THE LAUNDRY.
WHAT DO YOU THINK, AMERICA? OUR FIRST CALL IS FROM PORTLAND. JULIE. YOU'RE ON THE BOB BRAXTON SHOW.
BOB, YOU ARE SUCH A PIG. I DON'T BELIEVE WHAT I'M HEAR--
OH, YEAH? WELL, IT'S US "PIGS" WHO BRING HOME THE BACON. WHAT DO YOU SAY TO THAT, MIZZ FEMI-NITWIT? WHOOPS, CUT HER OFF. NEXT CALLER.
HEY, BOB. THIS IS GUS FROM HOUSTON, AND I THINK YOU'RE RIGHT ON THE BALL WITH THIS ONE.
MY WIFE'S BEEN GETTIN' PRETTY UPPITY LATELY, READIN' BOOKS AN' STUFF. THINKS MAYBE SHE OUGHTTA HAVE A CAREER OF HER OWN.
PUT YOUR FOOT DOWN, GUS! SHOW HER WHO'S THE MAN OF THE HOUSE!
DOCTOR, ARE YOU SURE YOU SHOULD KEEP THAT RADIO EQUIPMENT WITH HER? I THOUGHT S.T.A.R. LABS TOLD US TO--
SON, THIS PATIENT ISN'T GOING TO HURT ANYONE. S.T.A.R. LABS KEPT HER IN THAT RUBBER ROOM FOR MONTHS, AND SHE NEVER BUDGED AN INCH. SHE'S HARMLESS.
106
107
AND IF SHE'S GOT ANY WITS ABOUT HER AT ALL--
--SHE DESERVES TO HAVE A LITTLE ENTERTAIN-MENT, DON'T YOU THINK?
OUR NEXT CALL IS FROM GOTHAM CITY. ABE, GO AHEAD.
YOU ARE SO RIGHT! THOSE FEMINISTS ARE OUTTA CONTROL!

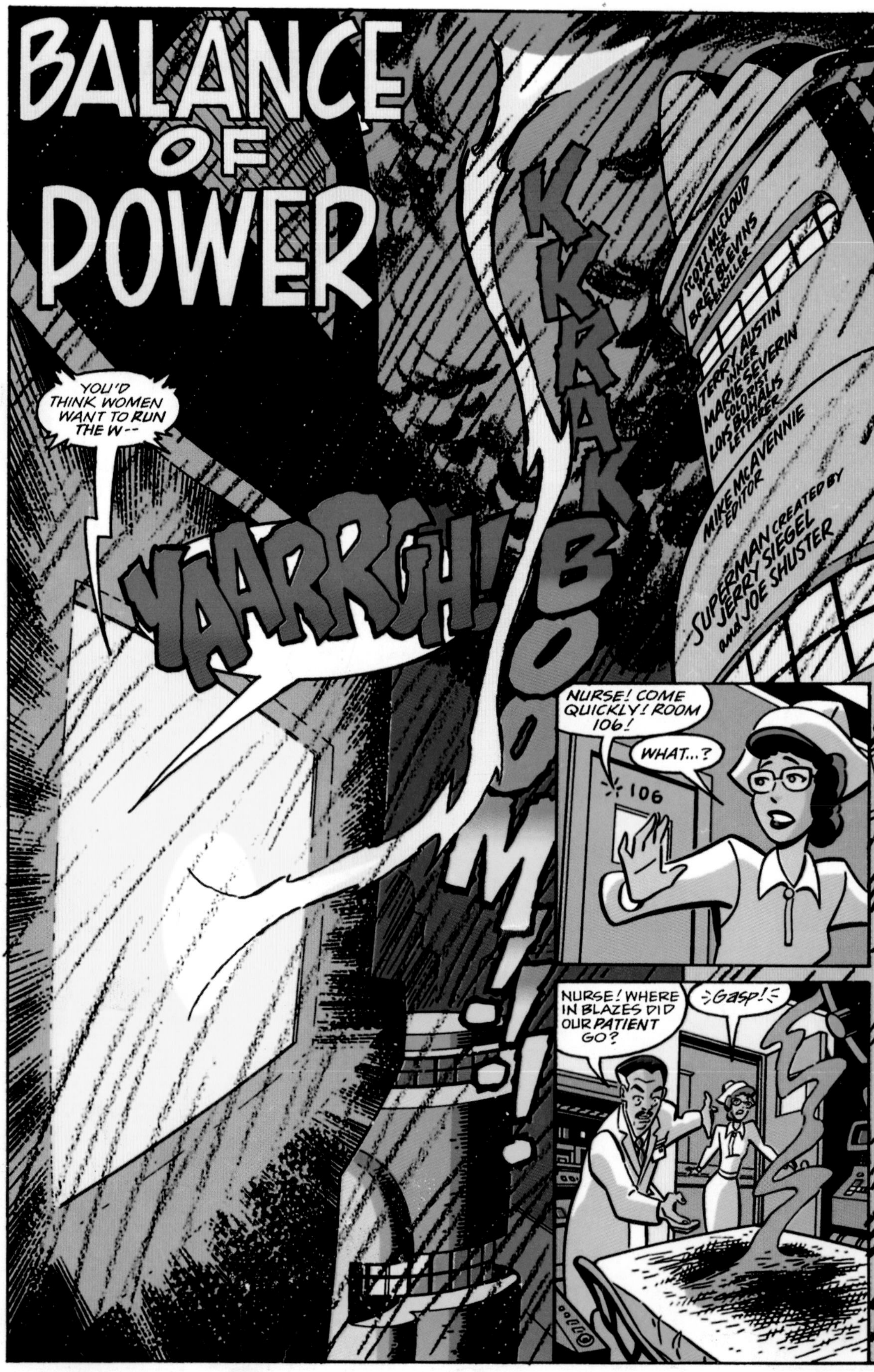
BALANCE OF POWER
SCOTT McCLOUD WRITER
BRET BLEVINS PENCILLER
TERRY AUSTIN INKER
MARIE SEVERIN COLORIST
LOIS BUHALIS LETTERER
MIKE McAVENNIE EDITOR
SUPERMAN CREATED BY JERRY SIEGEL and JOE SHUSTER
YOU'D THINK WOMEN WANT TO RUN THE W--
KKRAK
YAARRGH!
BOOM!!!
NURSE! COME QUICKLY! ROOM 106!
WHAT...?
106
NURSE! WHERE IN BLAZES DID OUR PATIENT GO?
Gasp!

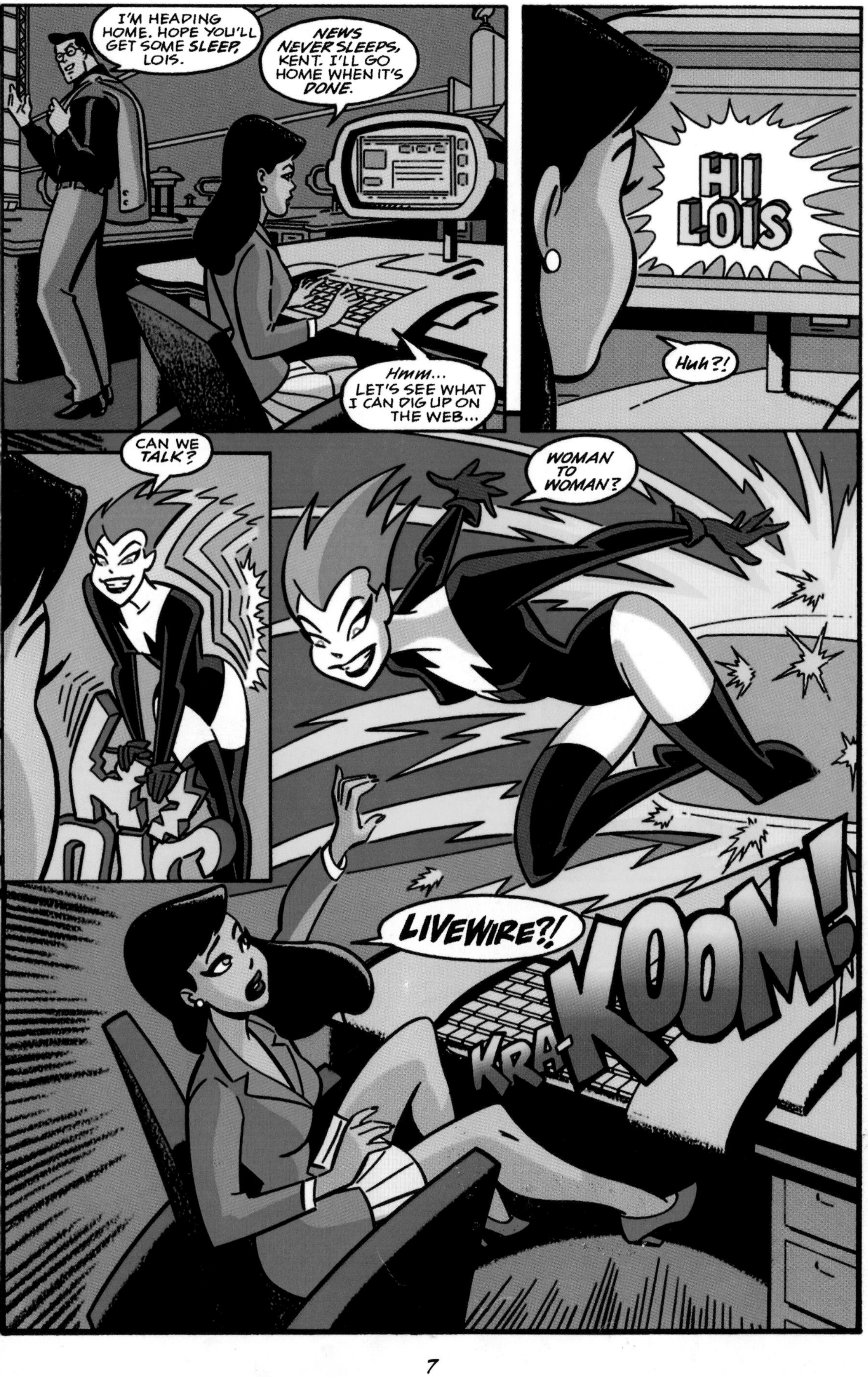
I'M HEADING HOME. HOPE YOU'LL GET SOME SLEEP, LOIS.
NEWS NEVER SLEEPS, KENT. I'LL GO HOME WHEN IT'S DONE.
Hmm... LET'S SEE WHAT I CAN DIG UP ON THE WEB...
HI LOIS
Huh?!
CAN WE TALK?
WOMAN TO WOMAN?
LIVEWIRE?!
KRA-KOOM!

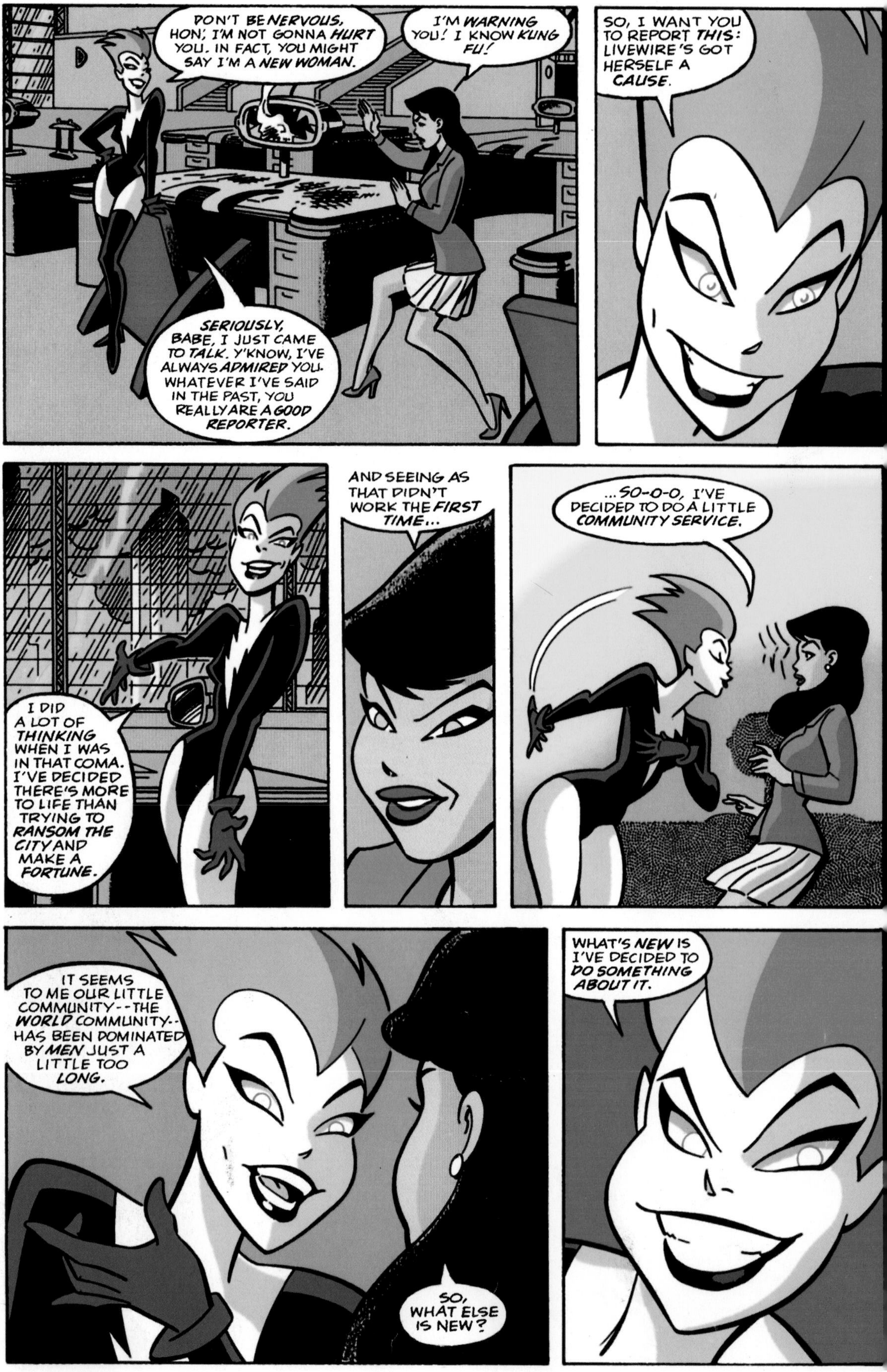
DON'T BE NERVOUS, HON; I'M NOT GONNA HURT YOU. IN FACT, YOU MIGHT SAY I'M A NEW WOMAN.
I'M WARNING YOU! I KNOW KUNG FU!
SERIOUSLY, BABE, I JUST CAME TO TALK. Y'KNOW, I'VE ALWAYS ADMIRED YOU. WHATEVER I'VE SAID IN THE PAST, YOU REALLY ARE A GOOD REPORTER.
SO, I WANT YOU TO REPORT THIS: LIVEWIRE'S GOT HERSELF A CAUSE.
I DID A LOT OF THINKING WHEN I WAS IN THAT COMA. I'VE DECIDED THERE'S MORE TO LIFE THAN TRYING TO RANSOM THE CITY AND MAKE A FORTUNE.
AND SEEING AS THAT DIDN'T WORK THE FIRST TIME...
...SO-O-O, I'VE DECIDED TO DO A LITTLE COMMUNITY SERVICE.
IT SEEMS TO ME OUR LITTLE COMMUNITY--THE WORLD COMMUNITY--HAS BEEN DOMINATED BY MEN JUST A LITTLE TOO LONG.
SO, WHAT ELSE IS NEW?
WHAT'S NEW IS I'VE DECIDED TO DO SOMETHING ABOUT IT.

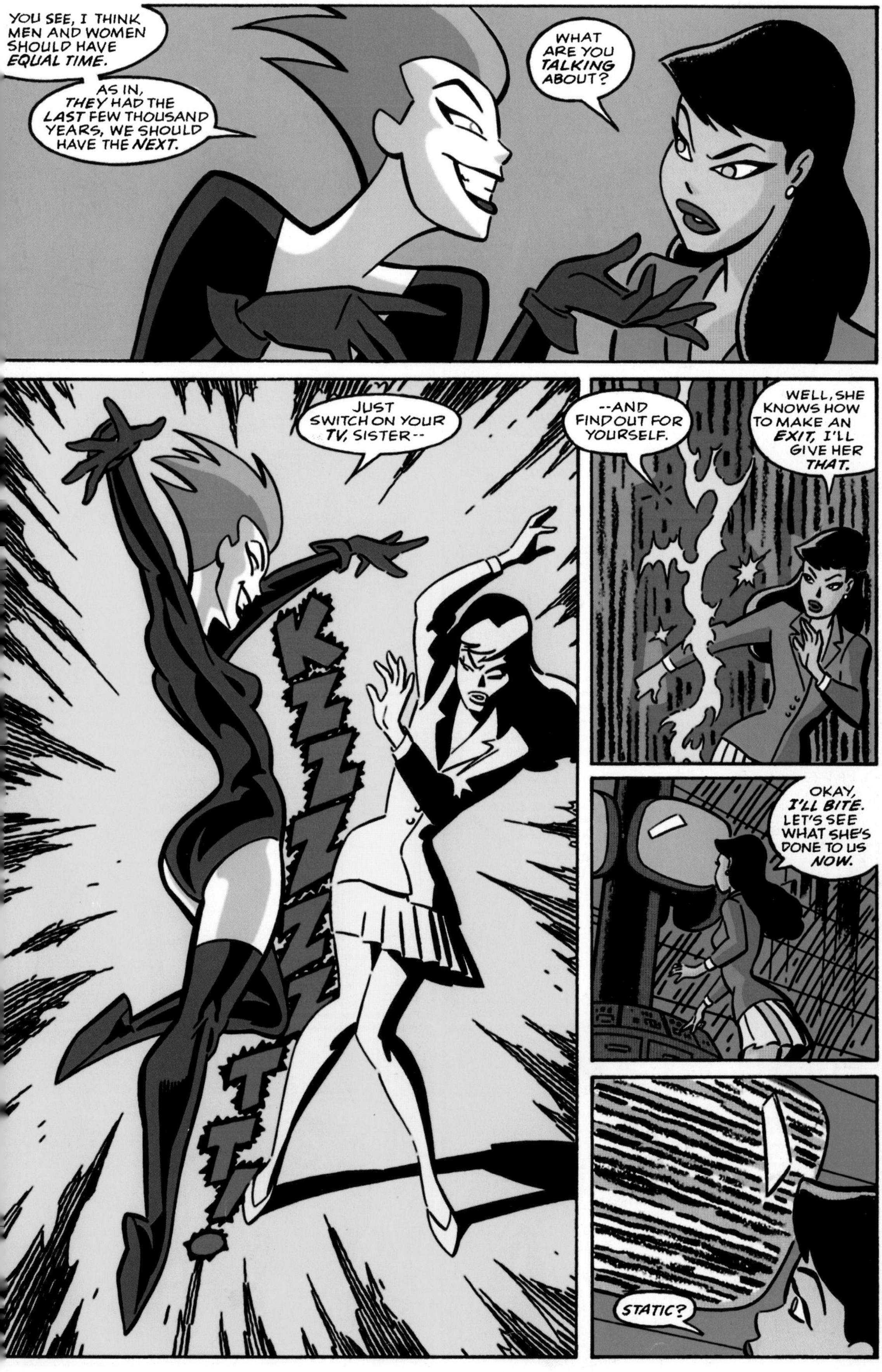
YOU SEE, I THINK MEN AND WOMEN SHOULD HAVE EQUAL TIME.
AS IN, THEY HAD THE LAST FEW THOUSAND YEARS, WE SHOULD HAVE THE NEXT.
WHAT ARE YOU TALKING ABOUT?
JUST SWITCH ON YOUR TV, SISTER--
KZZZZZZTTTT
--AND FIND OUT FOR YOURSELF.
WELL, SHE KNOWS HOW TO MAKE AN EXIT, I'LL GIVE HER THAT.
OKAY, I'LL BITE. LET'S SEE WHAT SHE'S DONE TO US NOW.
STATIC?

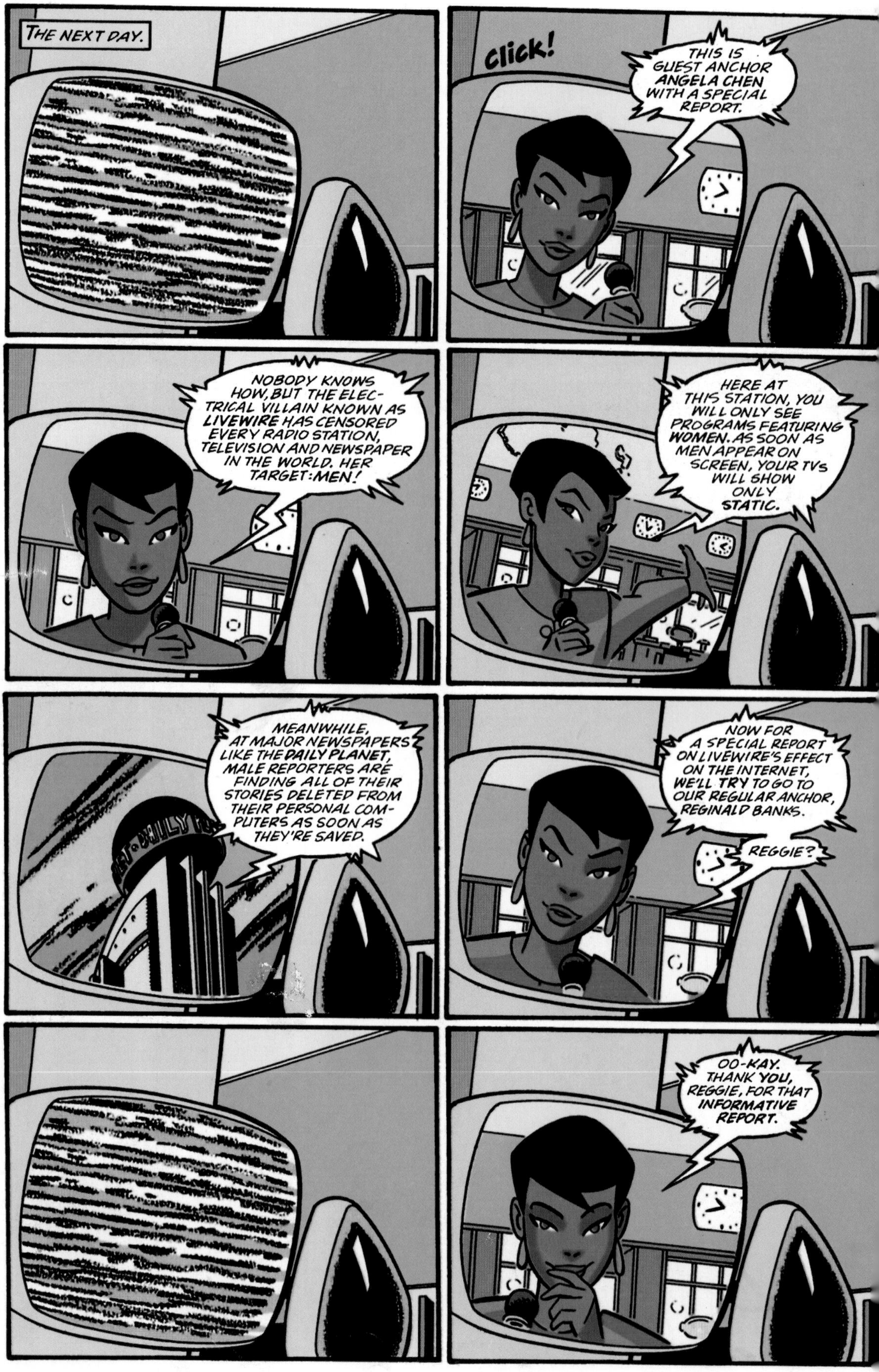
THE NEXT DAY.
CLICK!
THIS IS GUEST ANCHOR ANGELA CHEN WITH A SPECIAL REPORT.
NOBODY KNOWS HOW, BUT THE ELECTRICAL VILLAIN KNOWN AS LIVEWIRE HAS CENSORED EVERY RADIO STATION, TELEVISION AND NEWSPAPER IN THE WORLD. HER TARGET: MEN!
HERE AT THIS STATION, YOU WILL ONLY SEE PROGRAMS FEATURING WOMEN. AS SOON AS MEN APPEAR ON SCREEN, YOUR TVs WILL SHOW ONLY STATIC.
MEANWHILE, AT MAJOR NEWSPAPERS LIKE THE DAILY PLANET, MALE REPORTERS ARE FINDING ALL OF THEIR STORIES DELETED FROM THEIR PERSONAL COMPUTERS AS SOON AS THEY'RE SAVED.
NOW FOR A SPECIAL REPORT ON LIVEWIRE'S EFFECT ON THE INTERNET, WE'LL TRY TO GO TO OUR REGULAR ANCHOR, REGINALD BANKS.
REGGIE?
OO-KAY. THANK YOU, REGGIE, FOR THAT INFORMATIVE REPORT.

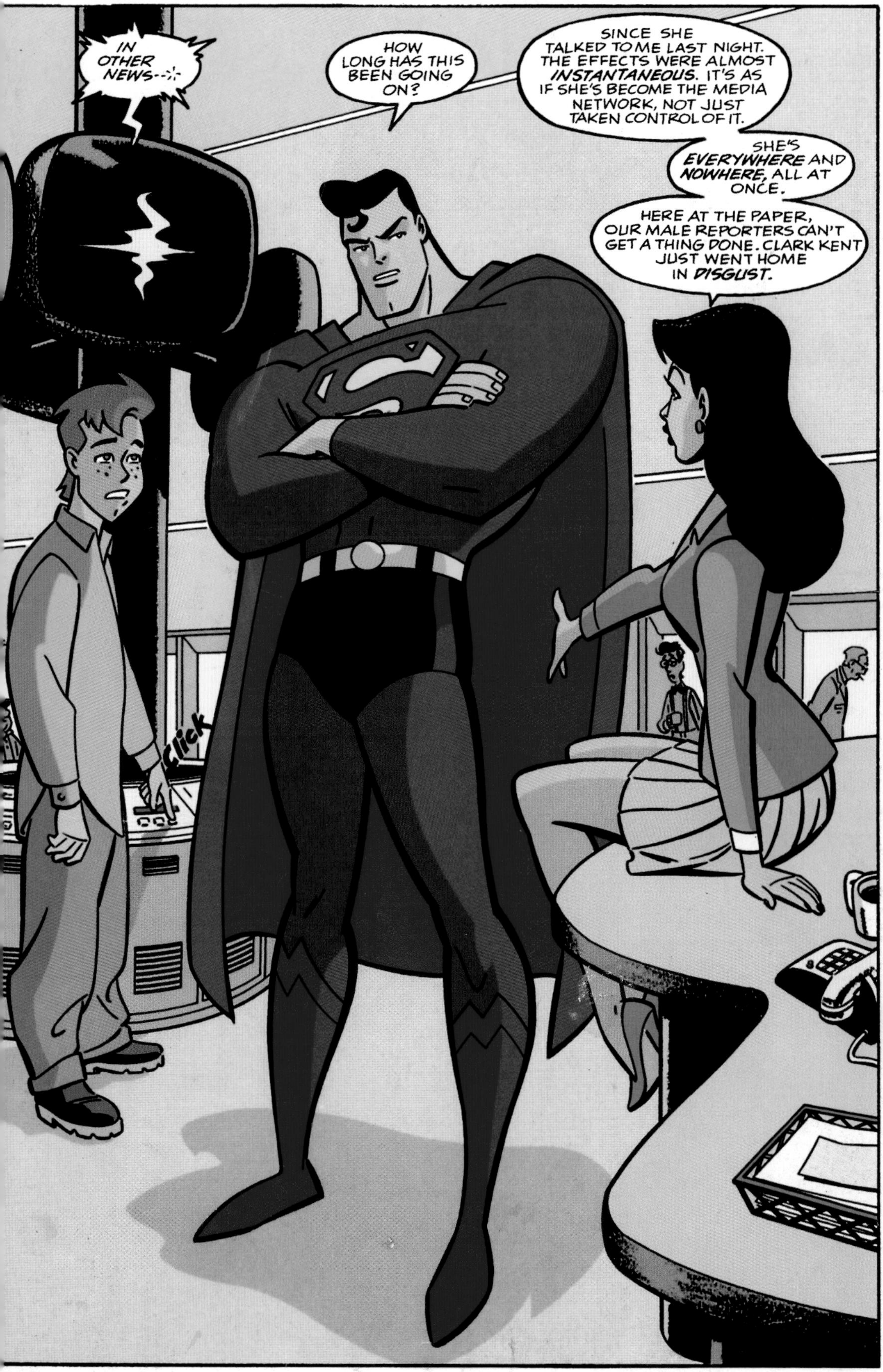
IN OTHER NEWS--
HOW LONG HAS THIS BEEN GOING ON?
SINCE SHE TALKED TO ME LAST NIGHT. THE EFFECTS WERE ALMOST *INSTANTANEOUS*. IT'S AS IF SHE'S BECOME THE MEDIA NETWORK, NOT JUST TAKEN CONTROL OF IT.
SHE'S *EVERYWHERE* AND *NOWHERE*, ALL AT ONCE.
HERE AT THE PAPER, OUR MALE REPORTERS CAN'T GET A THING DONE. CLARK KENT JUST WENT HOME IN *DISGUST*.
CLICK

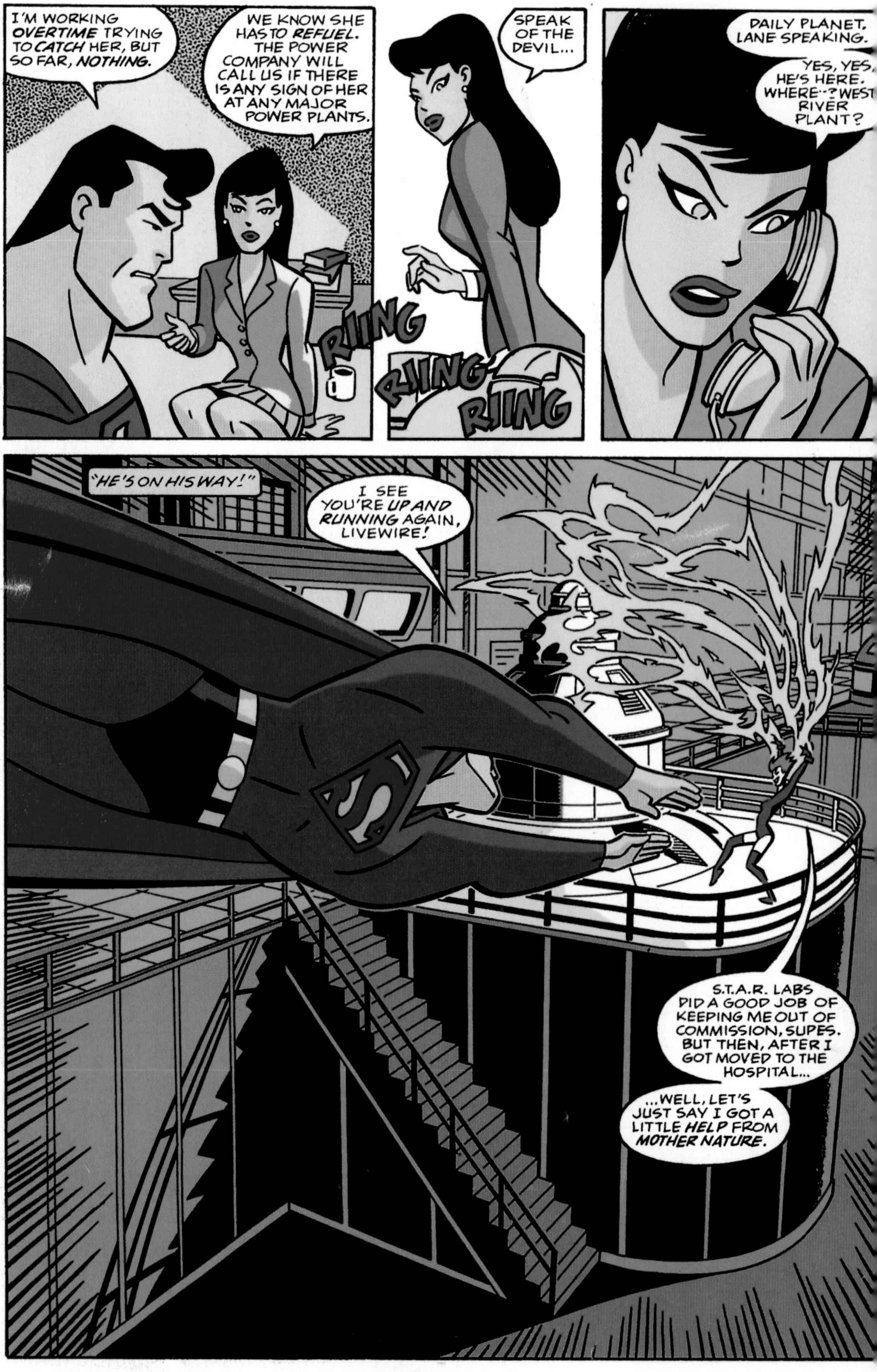
I'M WORKING OVERTIME TRYING TO CATCH HER, BUT SO FAR, NOTHING.
WE KNOW SHE HAS TO REFUEL. THE POWER COMPANY WILL CALL US IF THERE IS ANY SIGN OF HER AT ANY MAJOR POWER PLANTS.
RIIING
RIIING
RIIING
SPEAK OF THE DEVIL...
DAILY PLANET. LANE SPEAKING.
YES, YES, HE'S HERE. WHERE--? WEST RIVER PLANT?
"HE'S ON HIS WAY!"
I SEE YOU'RE UP AND RUNNING AGAIN, LIVEWIRE!
S.T.A.R. LABS DID A GOOD JOB OF KEEPING ME OUT OF COMMISSION, SUPES. BUT THEN, AFTER I GOT MOVED TO THE HOSPITAL...
...WELL, LET'S JUST SAY I GOT A LITTLE HELP FROM MOTHER NATURE.

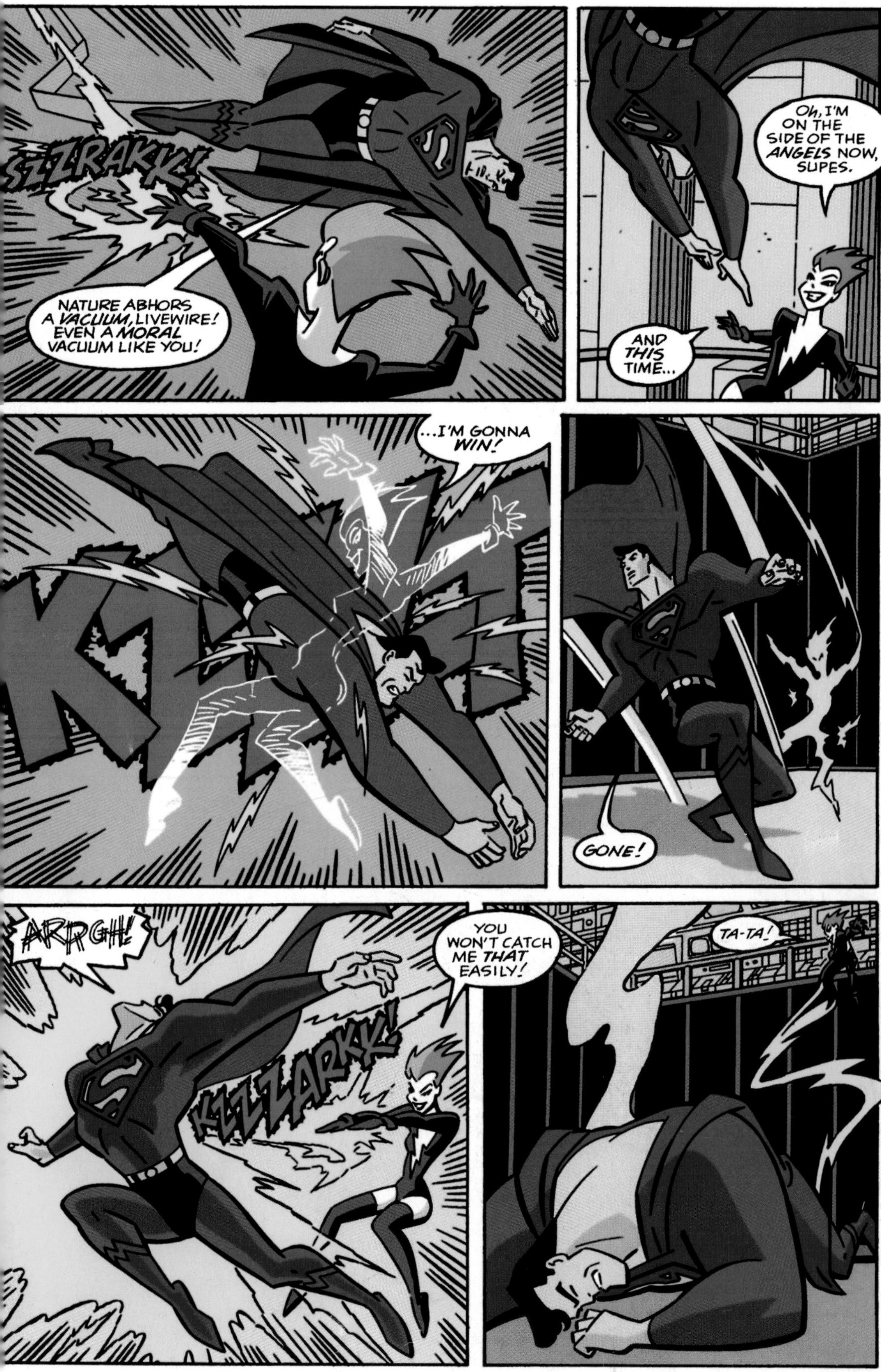
SZZRAKK!
NATURE ABHORS A VACUUM, LIVEWIRE! EVEN A MORAL VACUUM LIKE YOU!
Oh, I'M ON THE SIDE OF THE ANGELS NOW, SUPES.
AND THIS TIME...
...I'M GONNA WIN!
GONE!
ARRGH!
YOU WON'T CATCH ME THAT EASILY!
KZZZARKK!
TA-TA!

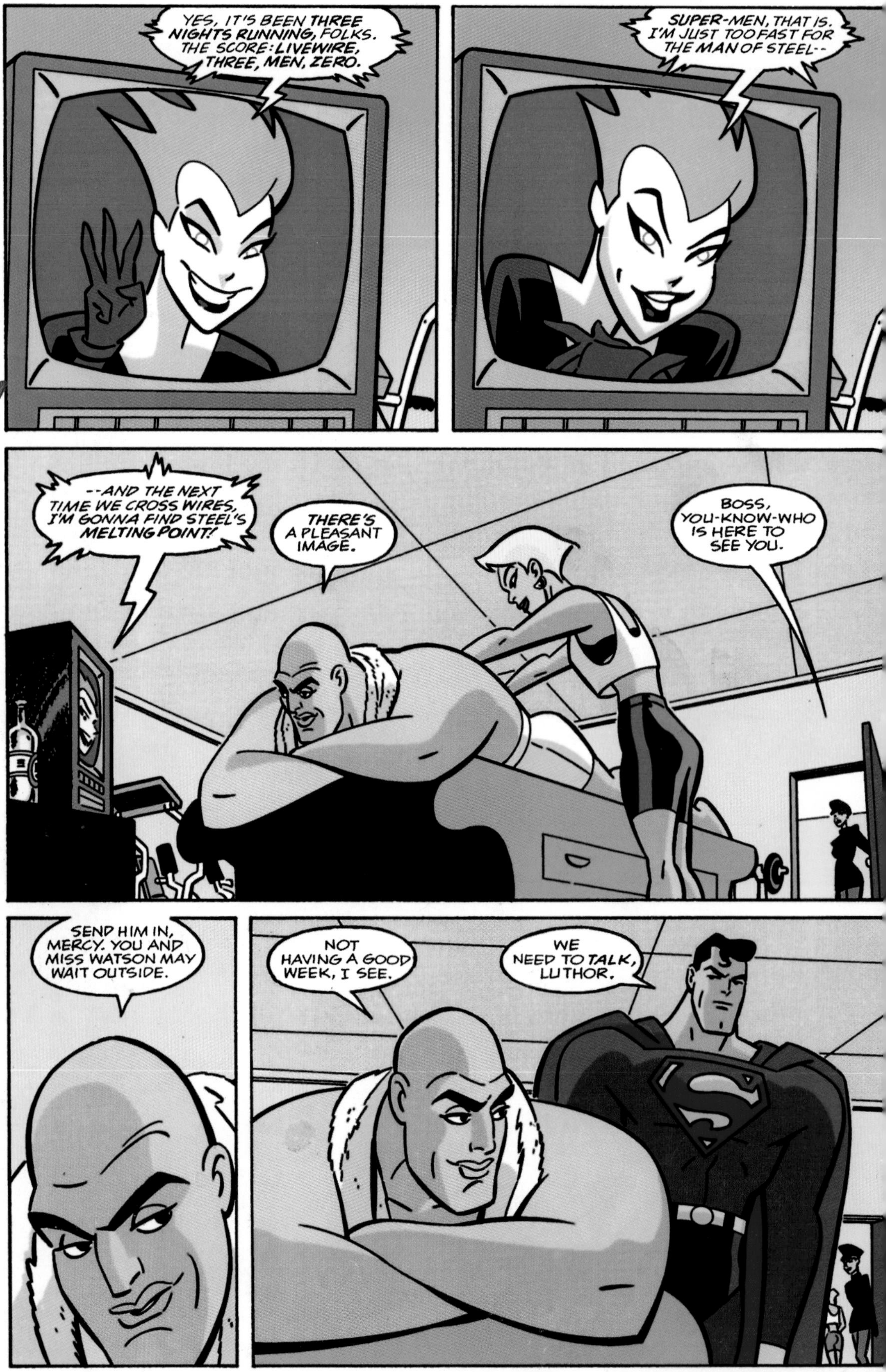
YES, IT'S BEEN THREE NIGHTS RUNNING, FOLKS. THE SCORE: LIVEWIRE, THREE, MEN, ZERO.
SUPER-MEN, THAT IS. I'M JUST TOO FAST FOR THE MAN OF STEEL--
--AND THE NEXT TIME WE CROSS WIRES, I'M GONNA FIND STEEL'S MELTING POINT!
THERE'S A PLEASANT IMAGE.
BOSS, YOU-KNOW-WHO IS HERE TO SEE YOU.
SEND HIM IN, MERCY. YOU AND MISS WATSON MAY WAIT OUTSIDE.
NOT HAVING A GOOD WEEK, I SEE.
WE NEED TO TALK, LUTHOR.

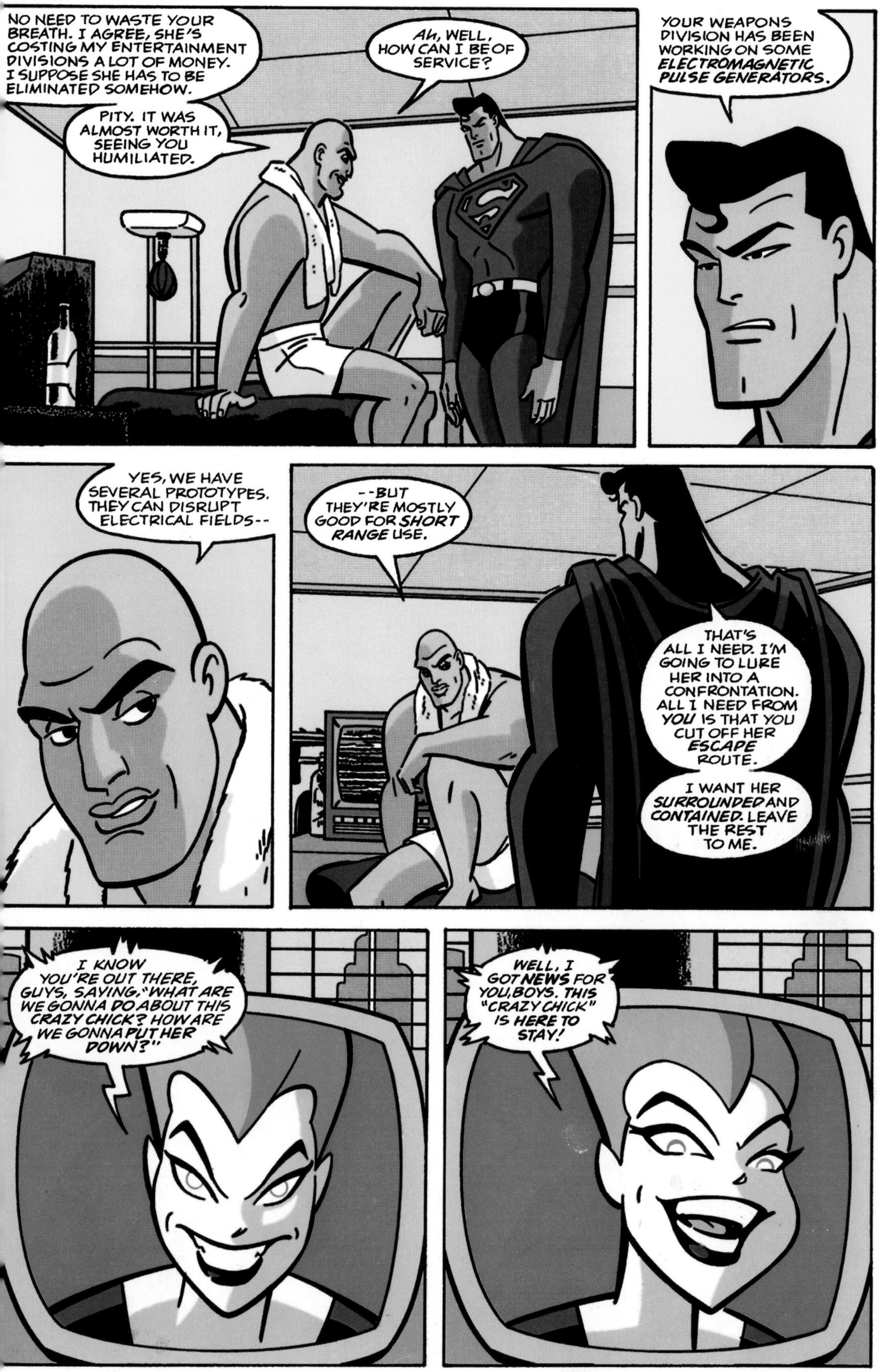
NO NEED TO WASTE YOUR BREATH. I AGREE, SHE'S COSTING MY ENTERTAINMENT DIVISIONS A LOT OF MONEY. I SUPPOSE SHE HAS TO BE ELIMINATED SOMEHOW.
PITY. IT WAS ALMOST WORTH IT, SEEING YOU HUMILIATED.
AH, WELL, HOW CAN I BE OF SERVICE?
YOUR WEAPONS DIVISION HAS BEEN WORKING ON SOME ELECTROMAGNETIC PULSE GENERATORS.
YES, WE HAVE SEVERAL PROTOTYPES. THEY CAN DISRUPT ELECTRICAL FIELDS--
--BUT THEY'RE MOSTLY GOOD FOR SHORT RANGE USE.
THAT'S ALL I NEED. I'M GOING TO LURE HER INTO A CONFRONTATION. ALL I NEED FROM YOU IS THAT YOU CUT OFF HER ESCAPE ROUTE.
I WANT HER SURROUNDED AND CONTAINED. LEAVE THE REST TO ME.
I KNOW YOU'RE OUT THERE, GUYS, SAYING, "WHAT ARE WE GONNA DO ABOUT THIS CRAZY CHICK? HOW ARE WE GONNA PUT HER DOWN?"
WELL, I GOT NEWS FOR YOU, BOYS. THIS "CRAZY CHICK" IS HERE TO STAY!

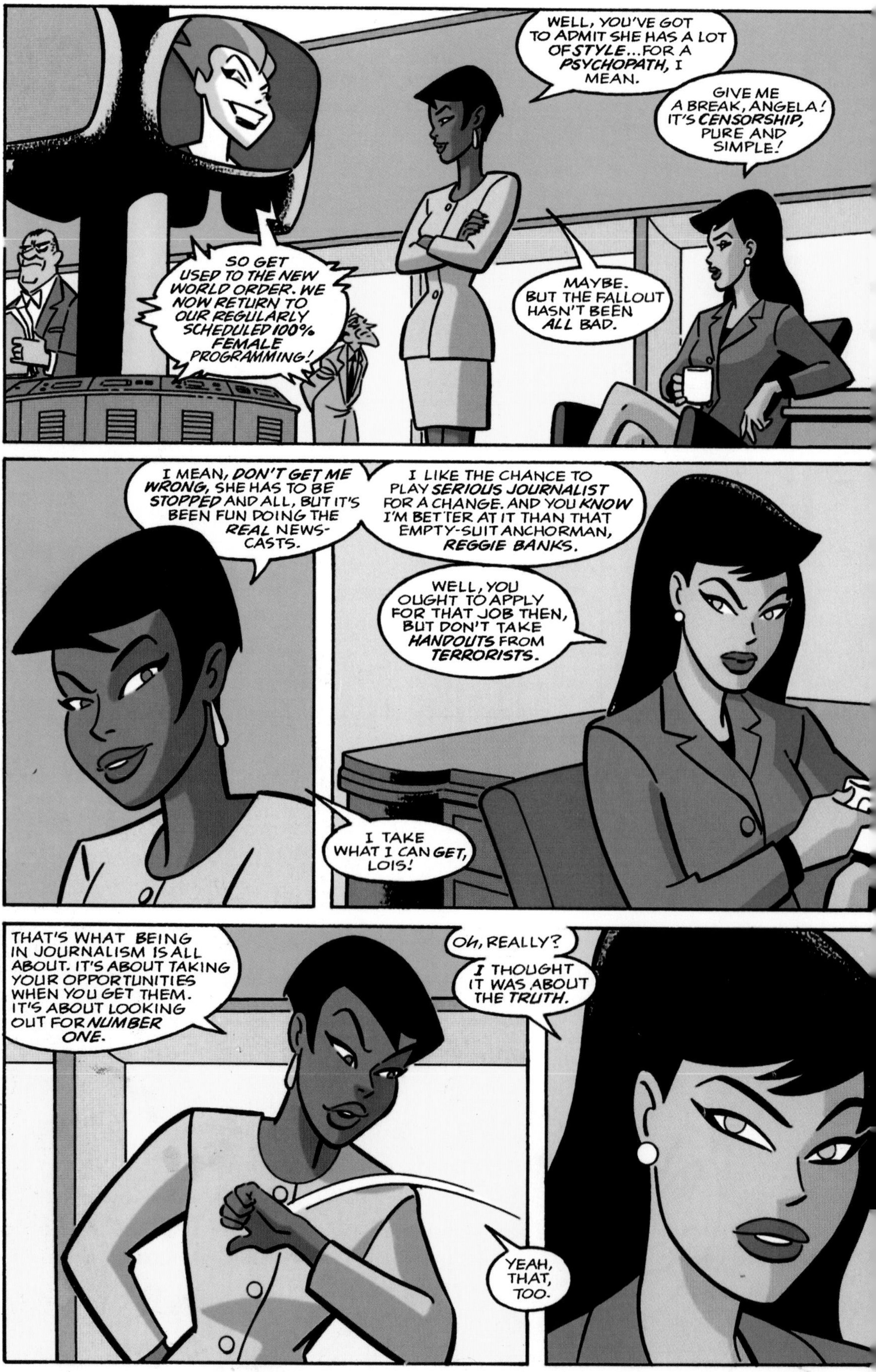
WELL, YOU'VE GOT TO ADMIT SHE HAS A LOT OF STYLE...FOR A PSYCHOPATH, I MEAN.
GIVE ME A BREAK, ANGELA! IT'S CENSORSHIP, PURE AND SIMPLE!
SO GET USED TO THE NEW WORLD ORDER. WE NOW RETURN TO OUR REGULARLY SCHEDULED 100% FEMALE PROGRAMMING!
MAYBE. BUT THE FALLOUT HASN'T BEEN ALL BAD.
I MEAN, DON'T GET ME WRONG, SHE HAS TO BE STOPPED AND ALL, BUT IT'S BEEN FUN DOING THE REAL NEWS-CASTS.
I LIKE THE CHANCE TO PLAY SERIOUS JOURNALIST FOR A CHANGE. AND YOU KNOW I'M BETTER AT IT THAN THAT EMPTY-SUIT ANCHORMAN, REGGIE BANKS.
WELL, YOU OUGHT TO APPLY FOR THAT JOB THEN, BUT DON'T TAKE HANDOUTS FROM TERRORISTS.
I TAKE WHAT I CAN GET, LOIS!
THAT'S WHAT BEING IN JOURNALISM IS ALL ABOUT. IT'S ABOUT TAKING YOUR OPPORTUNITIES WHEN YOU GET THEM. IT'S ABOUT LOOKING OUT FOR NUMBER ONE.
Oh, REALLY?
I THOUGHT IT WAS ABOUT THE TRUTH.
YEAH, THAT, TOO.

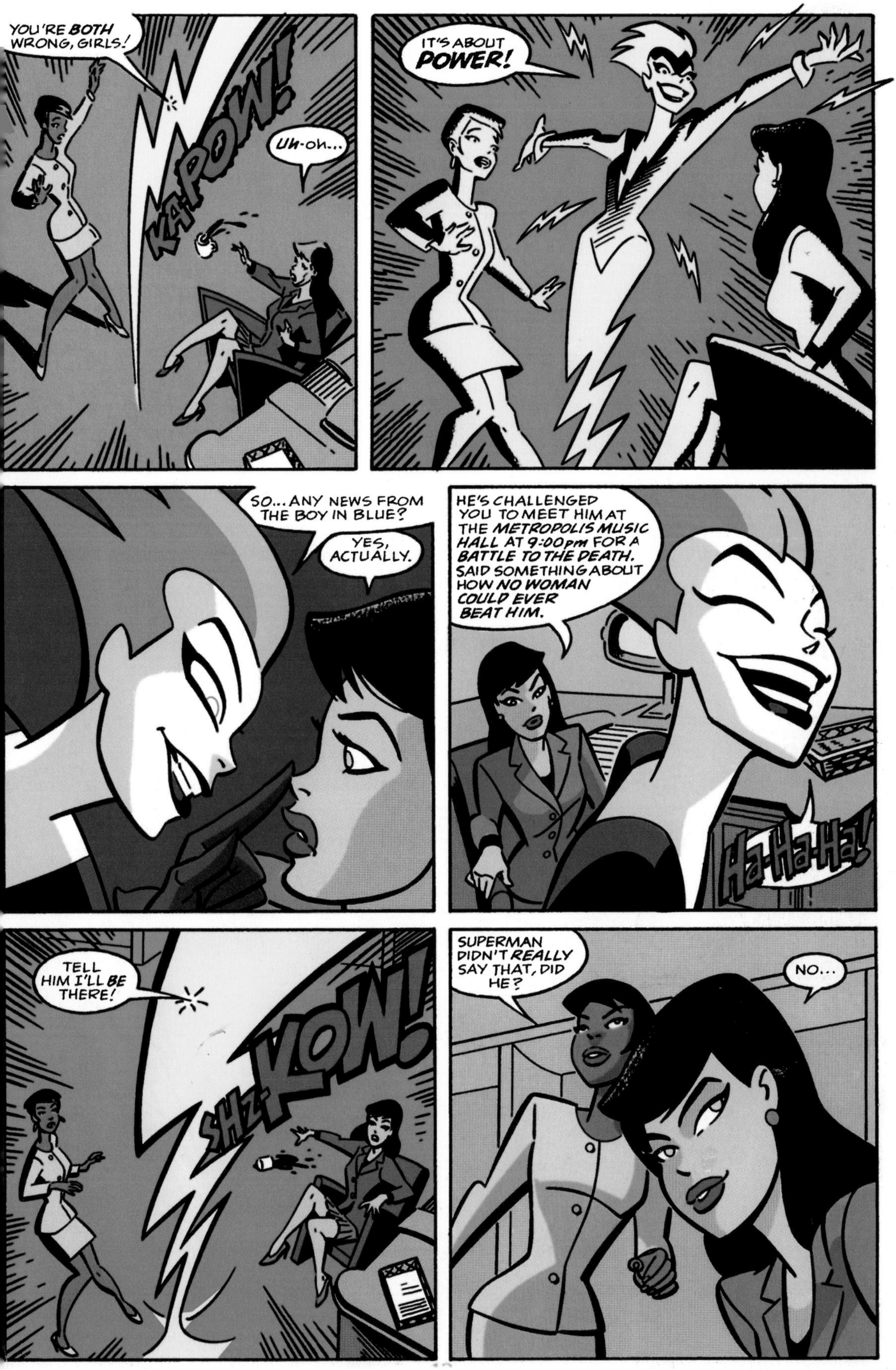
YOU'RE BOTH WRONG, GIRLS!
KA-POW!
Uh-oh...
IT'S ABOUT POWER!
SO... ANY NEWS FROM THE BOY IN BLUE?
YES, ACTUALLY.
HE'S CHALLENGED YOU TO MEET HIM AT THE METROPOLIS MUSIC HALL AT 9:00pm FOR A BATTLE TO THE DEATH. SAID SOMETHING ABOUT HOW NO WOMAN COULD EVER BEAT HIM.
Ha-Ha-Ha!
TELL HIM I'LL BE THERE!
SHZ-KOW!
SUPERMAN DIDN'T REALLY SAY THAT, DID HE?
NO...

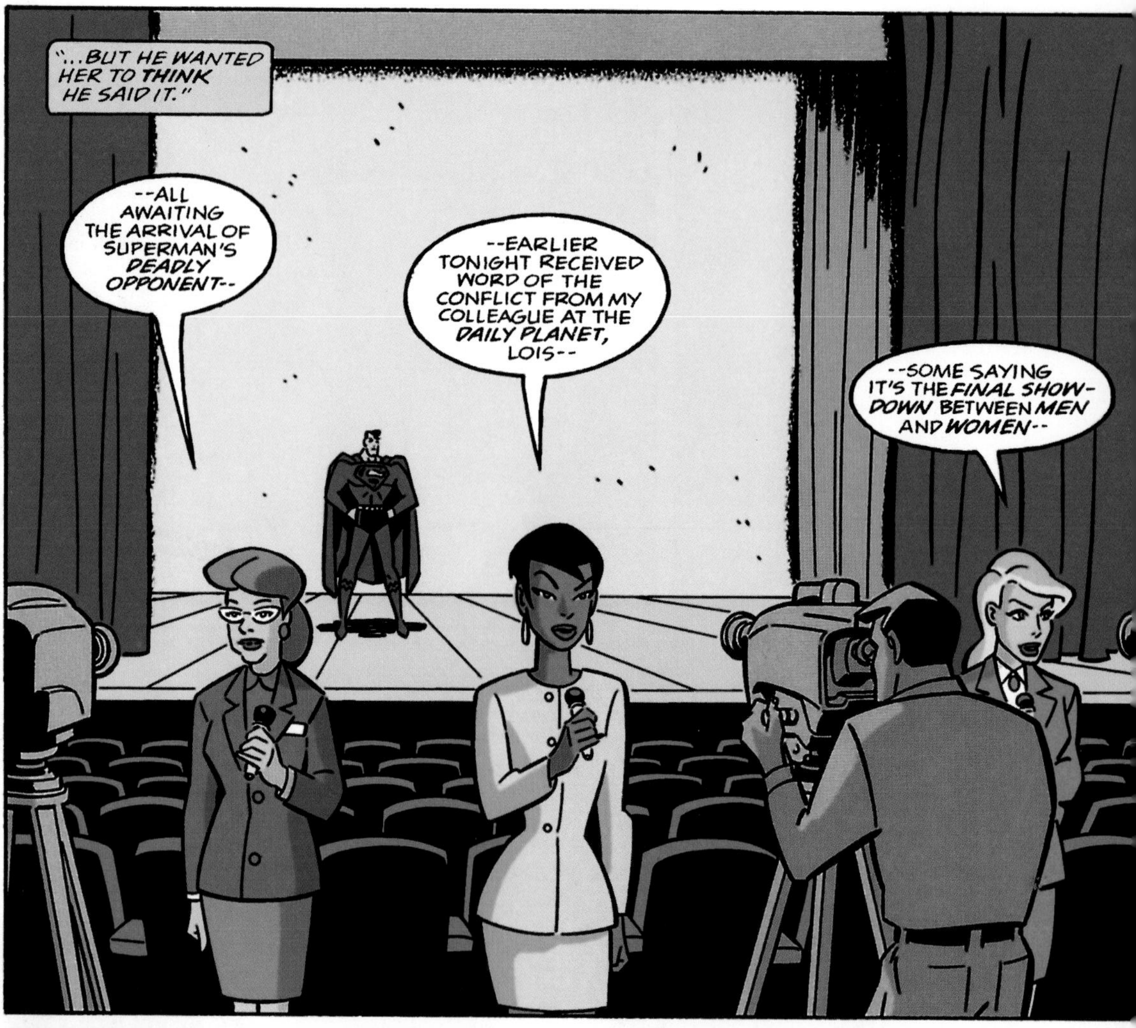
"...BUT HE WANTED HER TO THINK HE SAID IT."
--ALL AWAITING THE ARRIVAL OF SUPERMAN'S DEADLY OPPONENT--
--EARLIER TONIGHT RECEIVED WORD OF THE CONFLICT FROM MY COLLEAGUE AT THE DAILY PLANET, LOIS--
--SOME SAYING IT'S THE FINAL SHOW-DOWN BETWEEN MEN AND WOMEN--

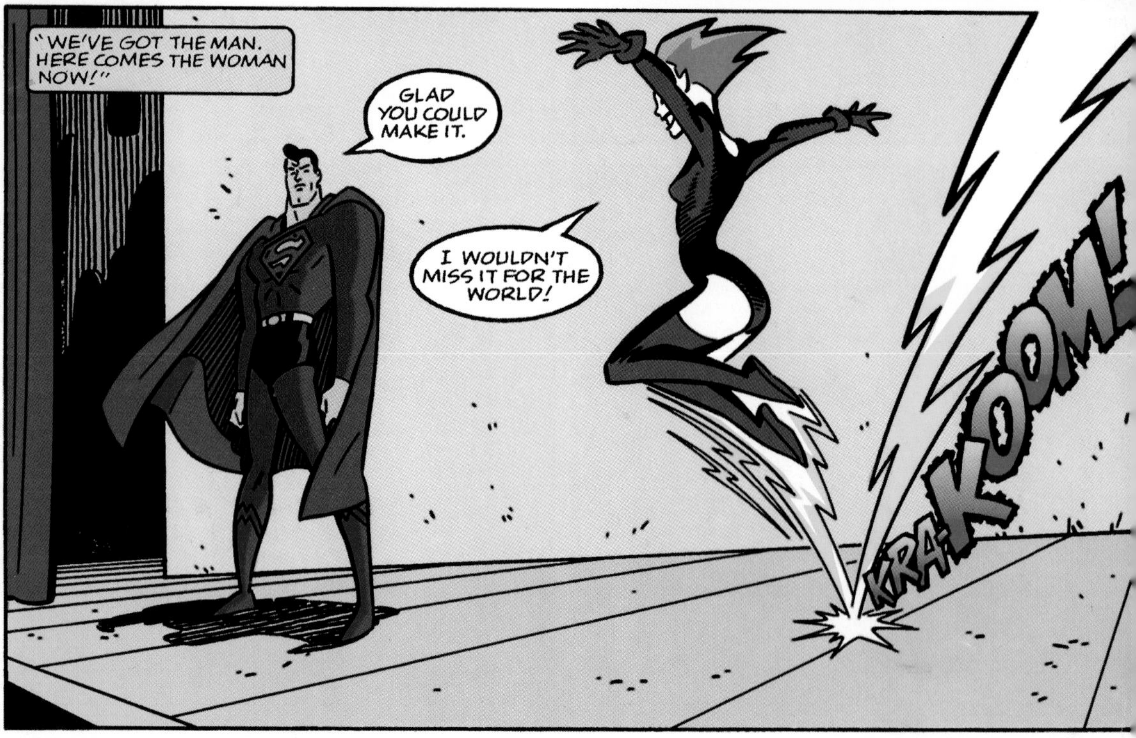
"WE'VE GOT THE MAN. HERE COMES THE WOMAN NOW!"
GLAD YOU COULD MAKE IT.
I WOULDN'T MISS IT FOR THE WORLD!
KRA-KOOM!

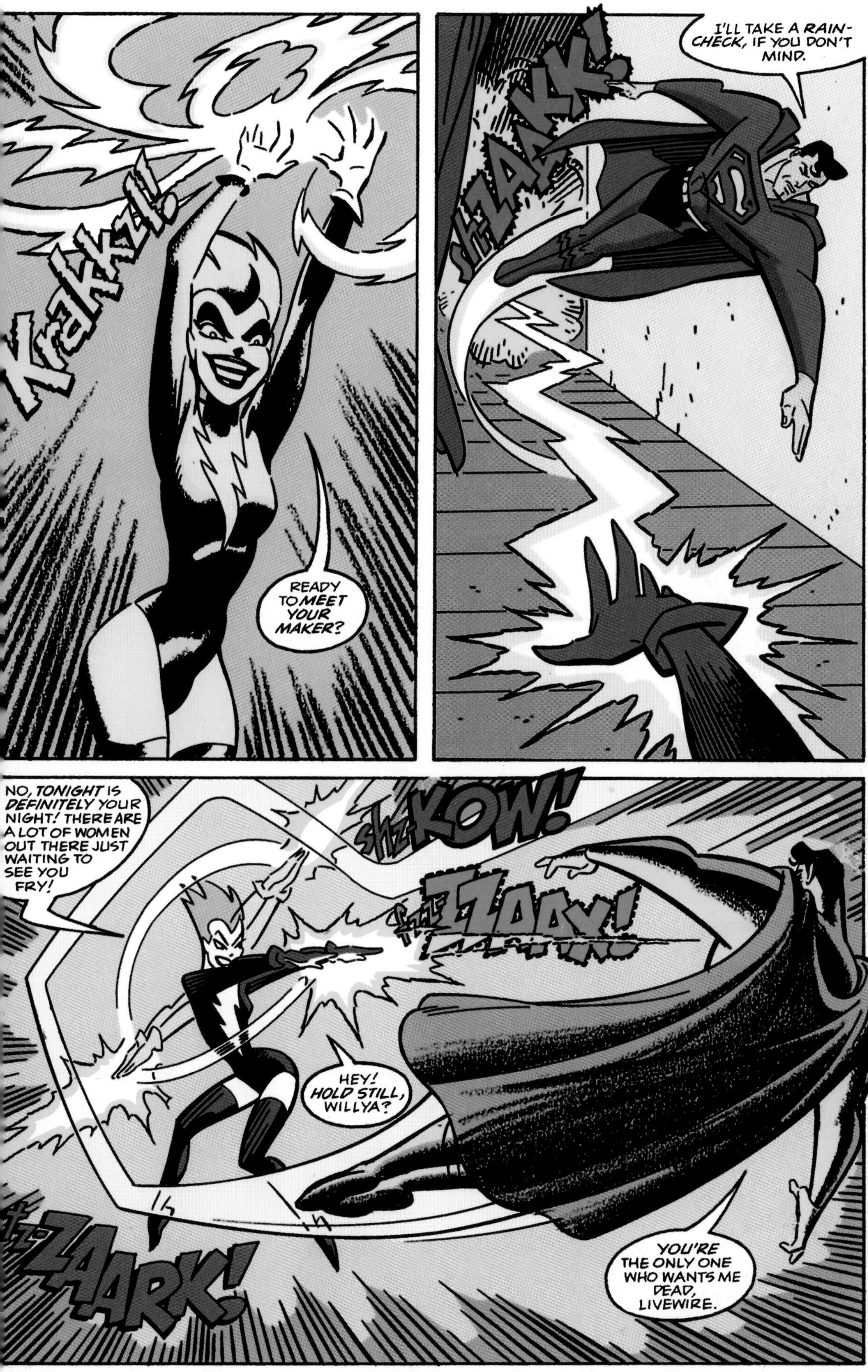
KRAKZZT!
READY TO MEET YOUR MAKER?
SHZAAKK!
I'LL TAKE A RAIN-CHECK, IF YOU DON'T MIND.
NO, TONIGHT IS DEFINITELY YOUR NIGHT! THERE ARE A LOT OF WOMEN OUT THERE JUST WAITING TO SEE YOU FRY!
SHZKOW!
FZZZAAK!
HEY! HOLD STILL, WILLYA?
TZZAARK!
YOU'RE THE ONLY ONE WHO WANTS ME DEAD, LIVEWIRE.

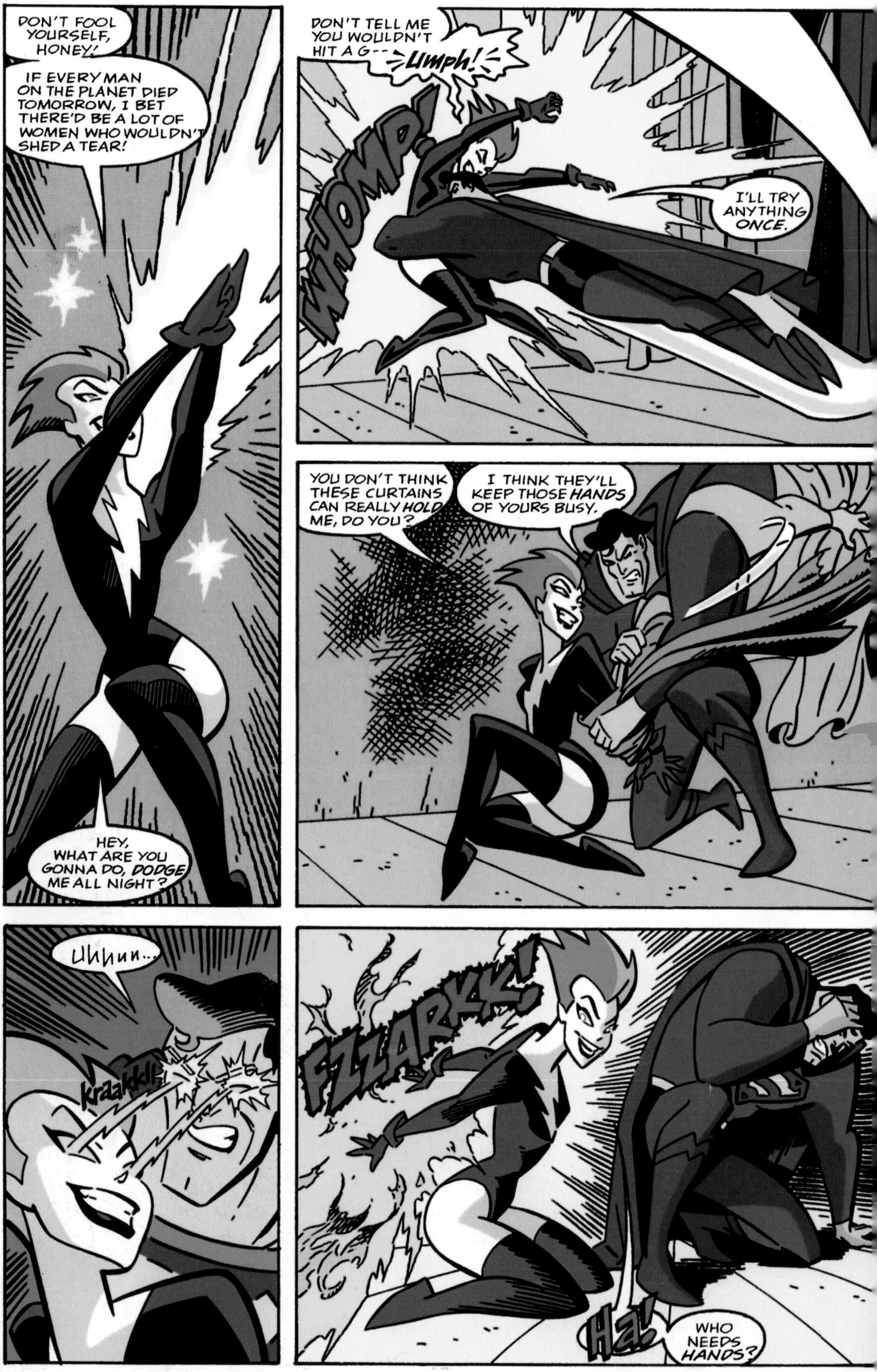
DON'T FOOL YOURSELF, HONEY!
IF EVERY MAN ON THE PLANET DIED TOMORROW, I BET THERE'D BE A LOT OF WOMEN WHO WOULDN'T SHED A TEAR!
HEY, WHAT ARE YOU GONNA DO, DODGE ME ALL NIGHT?
DON'T TELL ME YOU WOULDN'T HIT A G-- Umph!
WHOMP!
I'LL TRY ANYTHING ONCE.
YOU DON'T THINK THESE CURTAINS CAN REALLY HOLD ME, DO YOU?
I THINK THEY'LL KEEP THOSE HANDS OF YOURS BUSY.
Uhhnn...
KRAAKK!
FZZARKK!
HA!
WHO NEEDS HANDS?

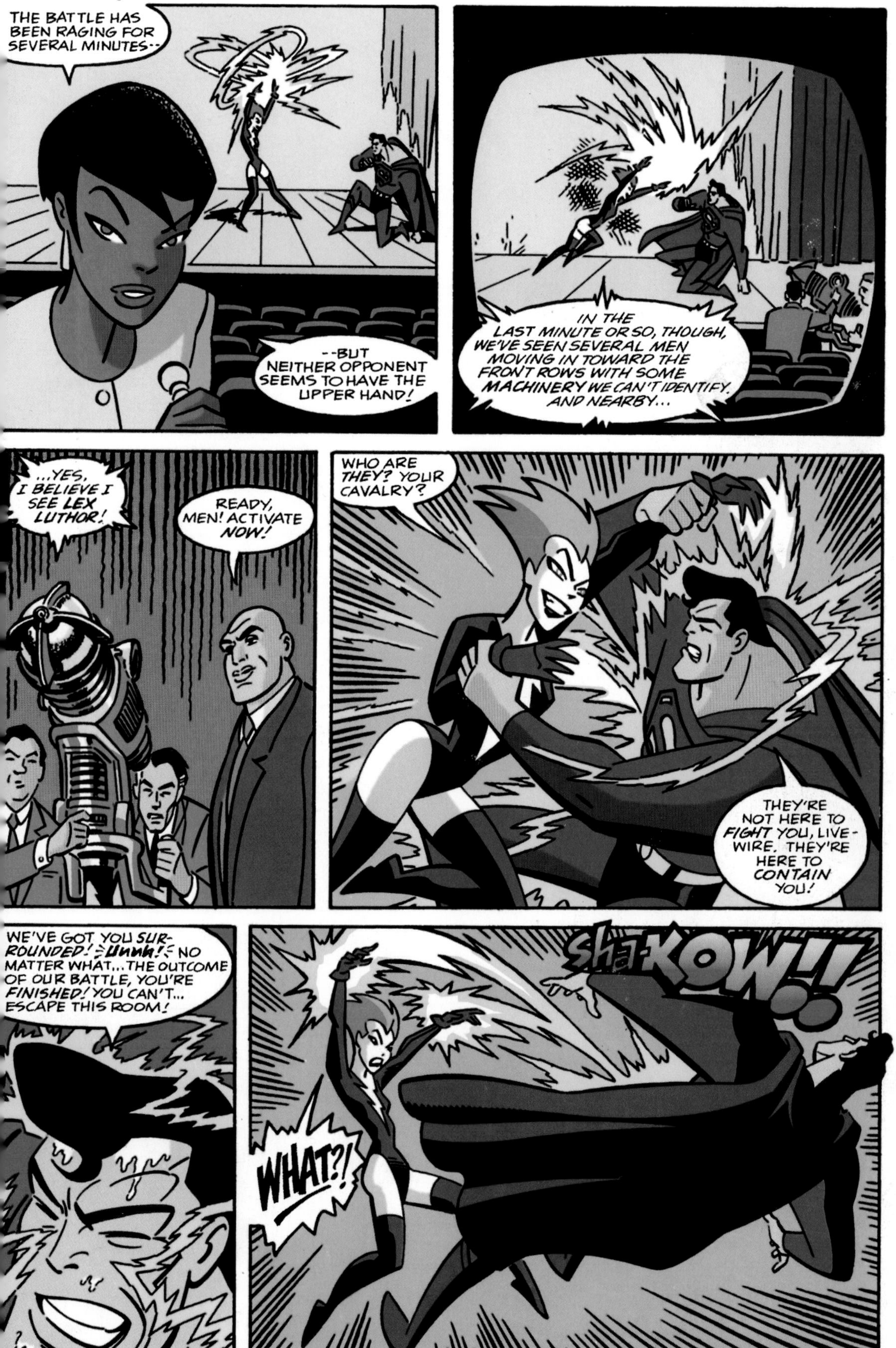
THE BATTLE HAS BEEN RAGING FOR SEVERAL MINUTES--
--BUT NEITHER OPPONENT SEEMS TO HAVE THE UPPER HAND!
IN THE LAST MINUTE OR SO, THOUGH, WE'VE SEEN SEVERAL MEN MOVING IN TOWARD THE FRONT ROWS WITH SOME MACHINERY WE CAN'T IDENTIFY. AND NEARBY...
...YES, I BELIEVE I SEE LEX LUTHOR!
READY, MEN! ACTIVATE NOW!
WHO ARE THEY? YOUR CAVALRY?
THEY'RE NOT HERE TO FIGHT YOU, LIVE-WIRE. THEY'RE HERE TO CONTAIN YOU!
WE'VE GOT YOU SUR-ROUNDED! Unnh! NO MATTER WHAT... THE OUTCOME OF OUR BATTLE, YOU'RE FINISHED! YOU CAN'T... ESCAPE THIS ROOM!
Sha-KOW!!
WHAT?!

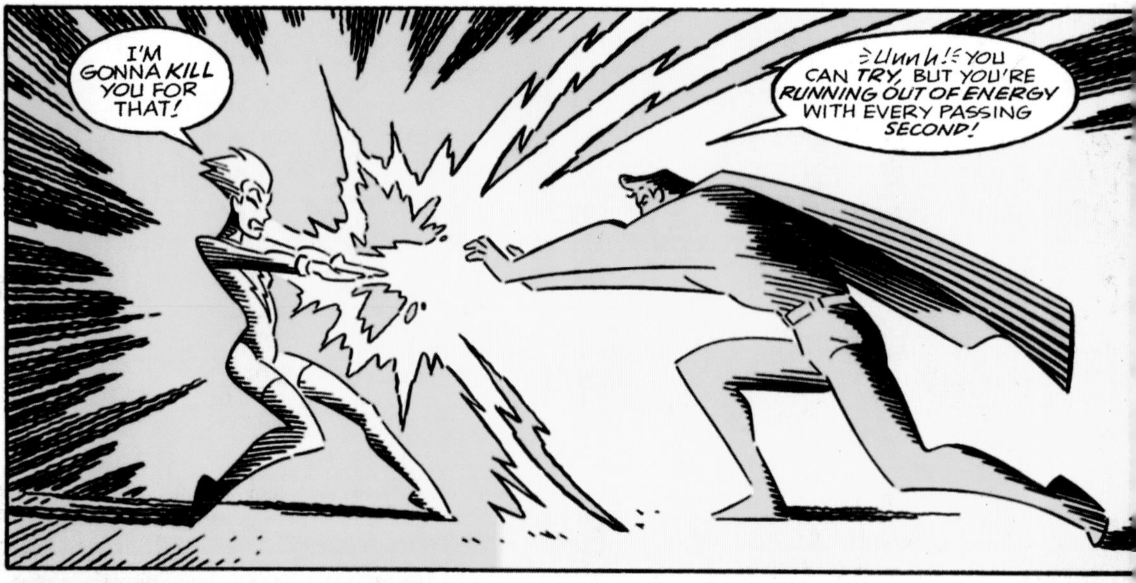
I'M GONNA KILL YOU FOR THAT!
Uunh! YOU CAN TRY, BUT YOU'RE RUNNING OUT OF ENERGY WITH EVERY PASSING SECOND!

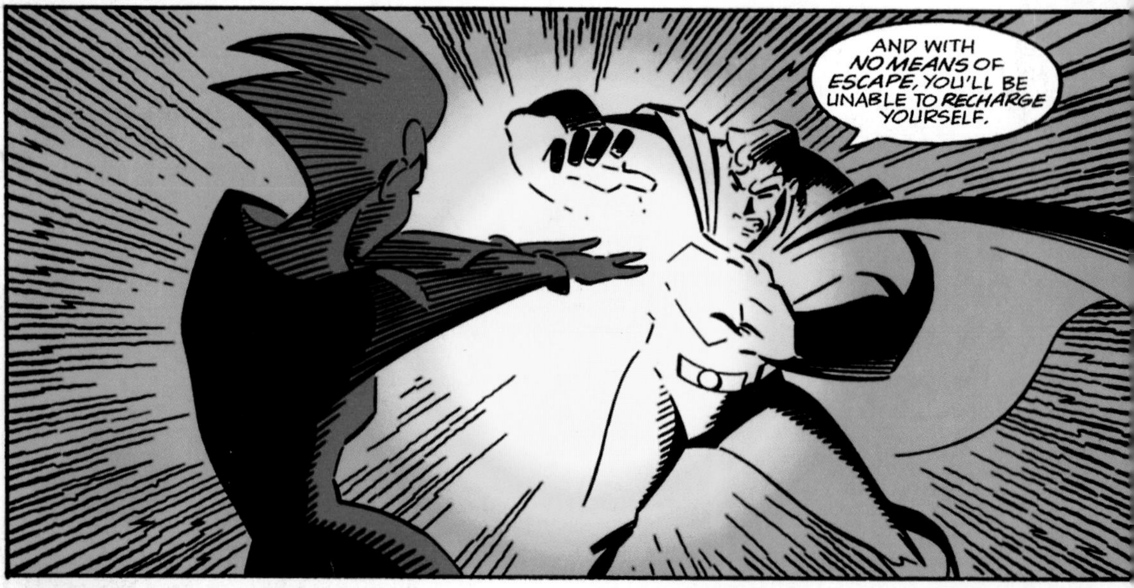
AND WITH NO MEANS OF ESCAPE, YOU'LL BE UNABLE TO RECHARGE YOURSELF.

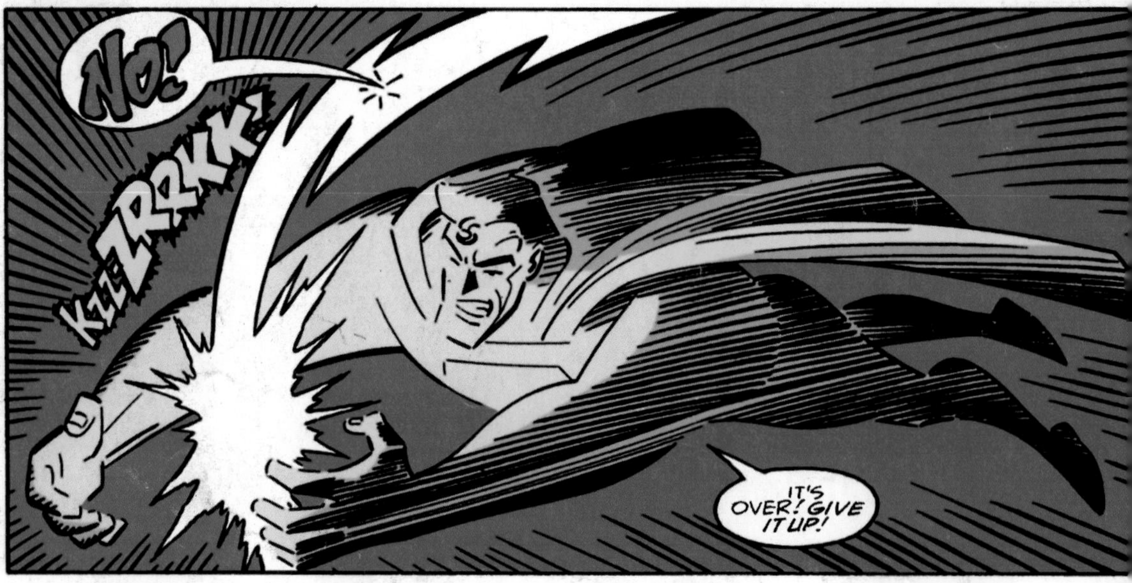
NO!
KZZZRRKK!
IT'S OVER! GIVE IT UP!

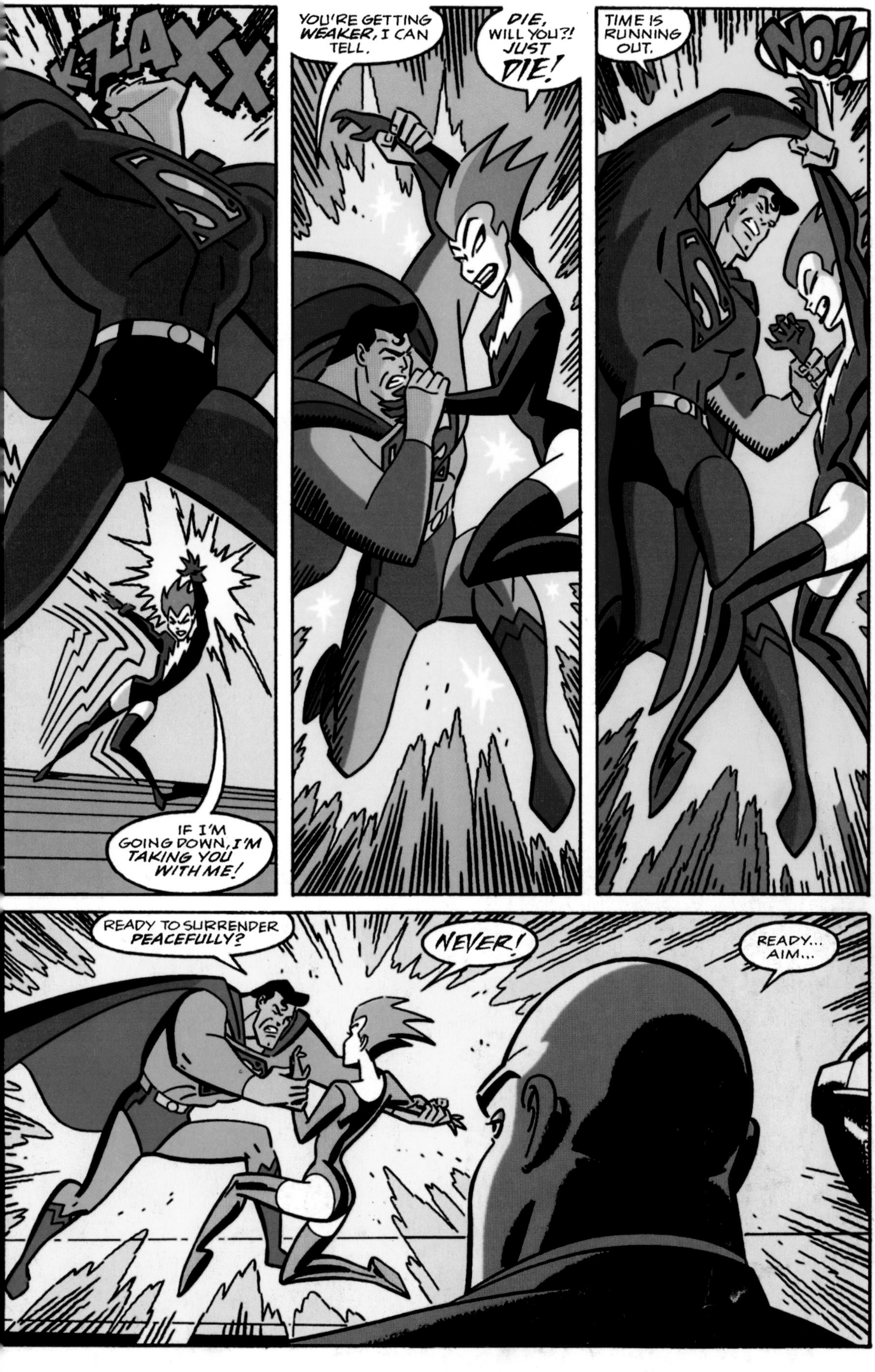
K-ZAXX
IF I'M GOING DOWN, I'M TAKING YOU WITH ME!
YOU'RE GETTING WEAKER, I CAN TELL.
DIE, WILL YOU?! JUST DIE!
TIME IS RUNNING OUT.
NO!!
READY TO SURRENDER PEACEFULLY?
NEVER!
READY... AIM...

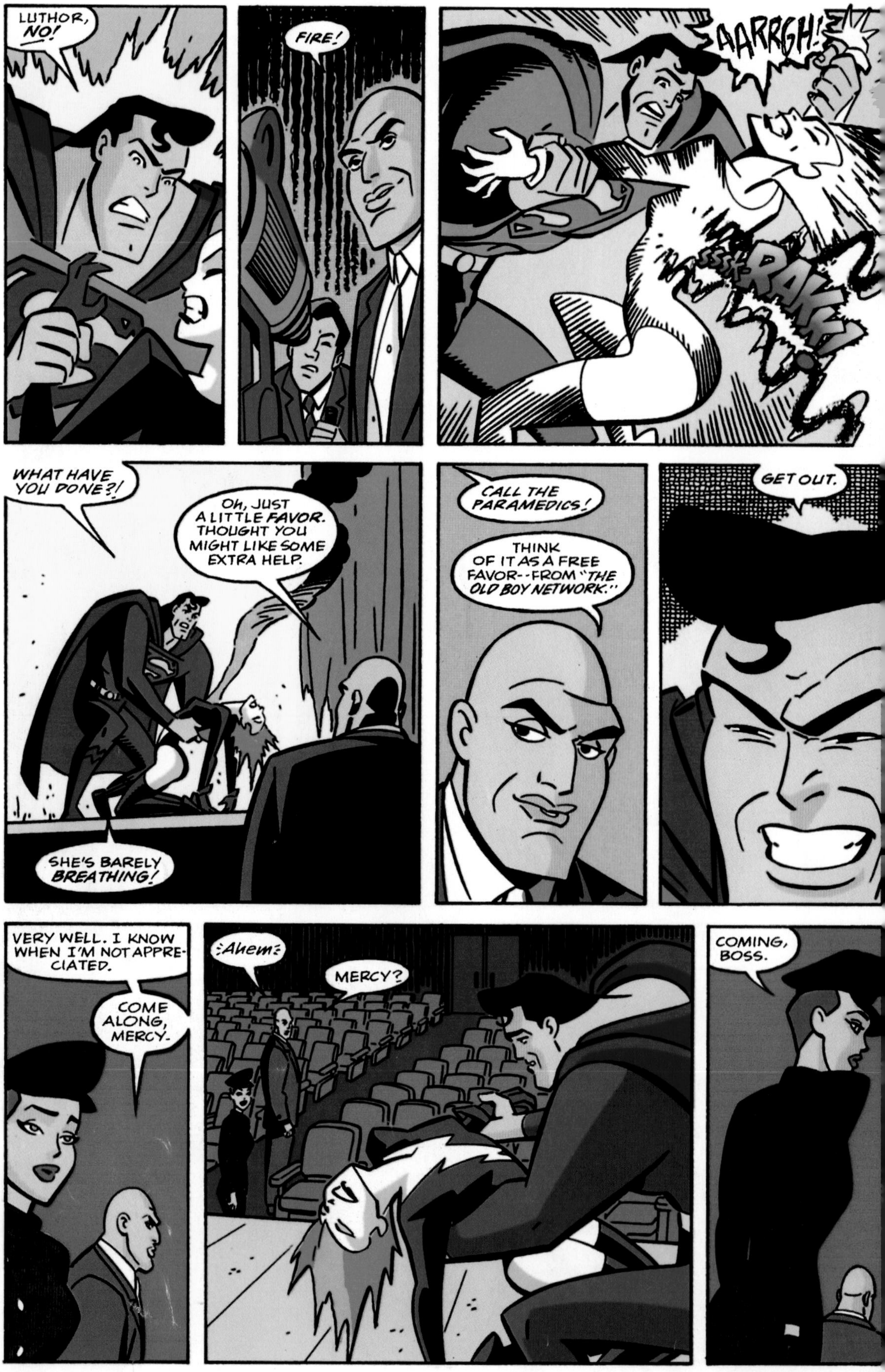

LUTHOR, NO!
FIRE!
AARRGH!
SSKRAKK!
WHAT HAVE YOU DONE?!
Oh, JUST A LITTLE FAVOR. THOUGHT YOU MIGHT LIKE SOME EXTRA HELP.
SHE'S BARELY BREATHING!
CALL THE PARAMEDICS!
THINK OF IT AS A FREE FAVOR--FROM "THE OLD BOY NETWORK."
GET OUT.
VERY WELL. I KNOW WHEN I'M NOT APPRECIATED.
COME ALONG, MERCY.
Ahem
MERCY?
COMING, BOSS.

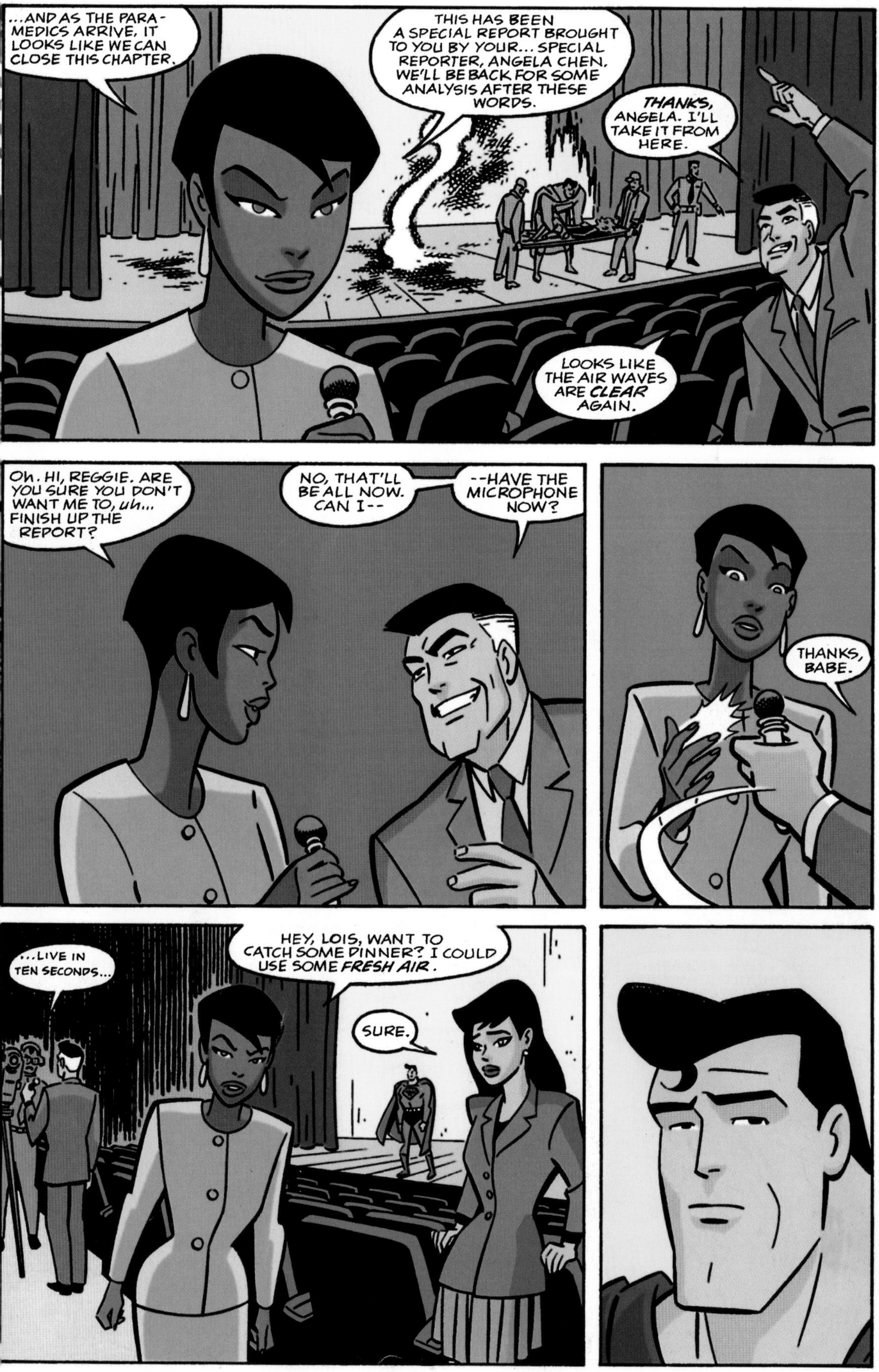

...AND AS THE PARA-MEDICS ARRIVE, IT LOOKS LIKE WE CAN CLOSE THIS CHAPTER.
THIS HAS BEEN A SPECIAL REPORT BROUGHT TO YOU BY YOUR... SPECIAL REPORTER, ANGELA CHEN. WE'LL BE BACK FOR SOME ANALYSIS AFTER THESE WORDS.
THANKS, ANGELA. I'LL TAKE IT FROM HERE.
LOOKS LIKE THE AIR WAVES ARE CLEAR AGAIN.
Oh. HI, REGGIE. ARE YOU SURE YOU DON'T WANT ME TO, uh... FINISH UP THE REPORT?
NO, THAT'LL BE ALL NOW. CAN I--
--HAVE THE MICROPHONE NOW?
THANKS, BABE.
...LIVE IN TEN SECONDS...
HEY, LOIS, WANT TO CATCH SOME DINNER? I COULD USE SOME FRESH AIR.
SURE.

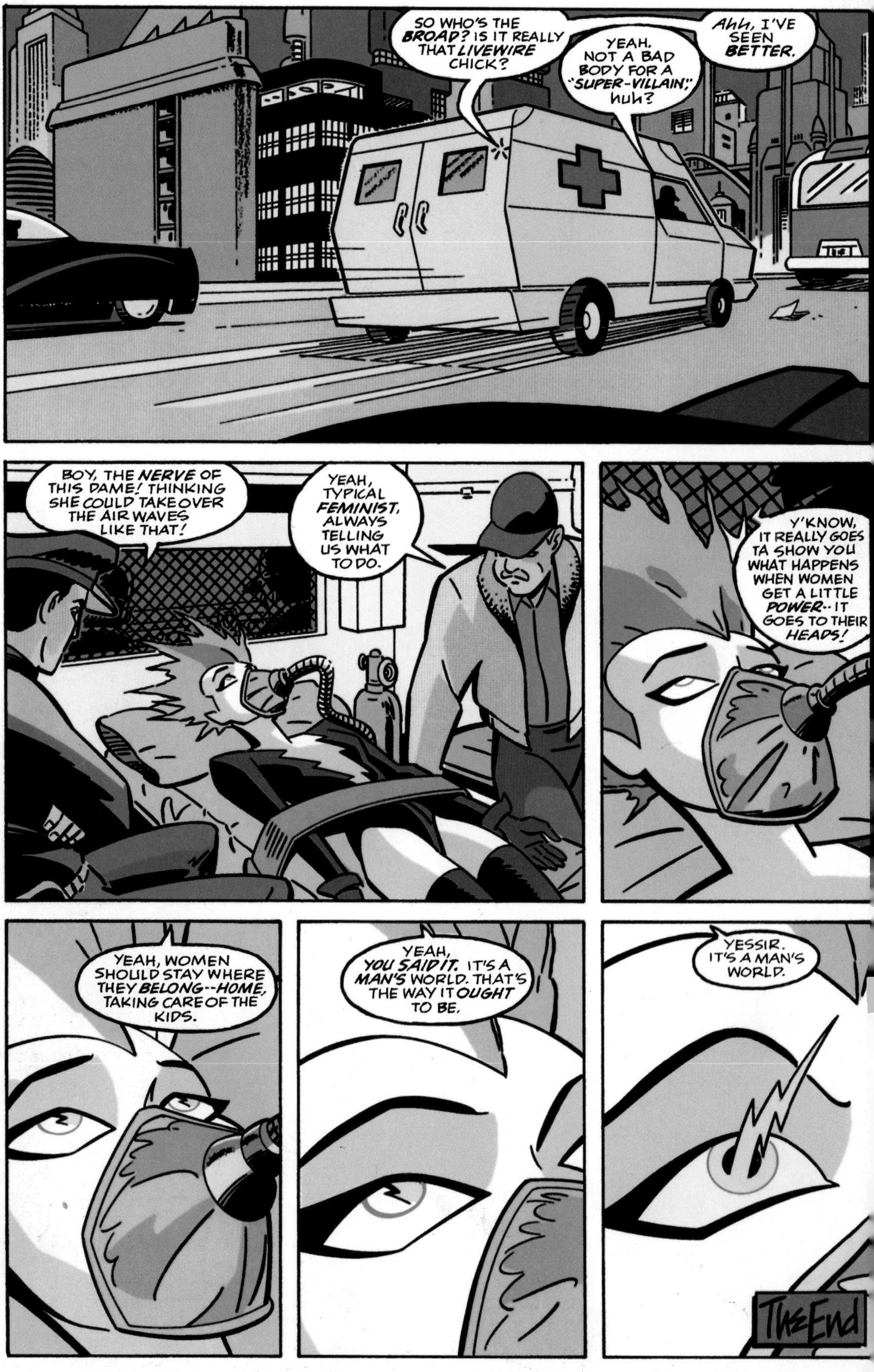
SO WHO'S THE BROAD? IS IT REALLY THAT LIVEWIRE CHICK?
YEAH. NOT A BAD BODY FOR A "SUPER-VILLAIN," HUH?
AHH, I'VE SEEN BETTER.
BOY, THE NERVE OF THIS DAME! THINKING SHE COULD TAKE OVER THE AIR WAVES LIKE THAT!
YEAH, TYPICAL FEMINIST, ALWAYS TELLING US WHAT TO DO.
Y'KNOW, IT REALLY GOES TA SHOW YOU WHAT HAPPENS WHEN WOMEN GET A LITTLE POWER-- IT GOES TO THEIR HEADS!
YEAH, WOMEN SHOULD STAY WHERE THEY BELONG--HOME, TAKING CARE OF THE KIDS.
YEAH, YOU SAID IT. IT'S A MAN'S WORLD. THAT'S THE WAY IT OUGHT TO BE.
YESSIR. IT'S A MAN'S WORLD.
The End

CREATORS

SCOTT McCLOUD *WRITER*

Scott McCloud is an acclaimed comics creator and author whose best-known work is the graphic novel *Understanding Comics*. His work also includes the science-fiction adventure series *Zot!*, a 12-issue run of *Superman Adventures*, and much more. Scott is the creator of the "24 Hour Comic," and frequently lectures on comics theory.

BRET BLEVINS *PENCILLER*

Bret Blevins is a professional comic book and animation artist. He has worked with today's top publishers and animation studios, including DC Comics, Marvel, Dark Horse, Disney, and Warner Bros. He has illustrated some of the world's best-known characters, like Batman, Superman, the Incredible Hulk, and more!

TERRY AUSTIN *INKER*

Throughout his career, inker Terry Austin has received dozens of awards for his work on high-profile comics for DC Comics and Marvel, such as *The Uncanny X-Men*, *Doctor Strange*, *Justice League America*, *Green Lantern*, and *Superman Adventures*. He lives near Poughkeepsie, New York.

GLOSSARY

admirer (ad-MIRE-ur)--one who likes or respects another

censored (SEN-surd)--banned from sight or use due to objectionable material

disgust (diss-GHUST)--to offend good taste or moral sense

dominated (DOM-uh-nay-tid)--controlled or ruled

fallout (FAWL-out)--the result of an action

feminist (FEM-uh-nist)--someone who believes strongly that women ought to have equal rights and opportunities that men have

instantaneous (in-stuhn-TAY-nee-uhss)--occuring, done, or completed in an instant

lure (LOOR)--to attract and perhaps lead someone or some creature into a trap

machinery (muh-SHEE-nuh-ree)--a group of machines, or parts of a machine

prototype (PROH-tuh-type)--an original model on which something is patterned

ransom (RAN-suhm)--money that is demanded before someone who is being held captive can be set free

surrender (suh-REN-dur)--to give up, or admit that you are beaten in a fight or battle

SUPERMAN GLOSSARY

Clark Kent: Superman's alter ego, Clark Kent, is a reporter for the *Daily Planet* newspaper and was raised by Ma and Pa Kent. No one knows he is Superman except for his adopted parents, the Kents.

The Daily Planet: the city of Metropolis's biggest and most read newspaper. Clark, Lois, Jimmy, and Perry all work for the Daily Planet.

Lex Luthor: Lex believes Superman is a threat to Earth and must be stopped. He will do anything it takes to bring the Man of Steel to his knees.

Livewire: Livewire can absorb and release electrical energy up to extremely high voltages. She can also transform into living energy and seemingly teleport across power lines and other sources of electricity.

Lois Lane: like Clark Kent, Lois is a reporter at the Daily Planet. She is also one of Clark's best friends.

Mercy Graves: Mercy is Lex Luthor's personal assistant and bodyguard. She is fiercely loyal to Lex and is never far from his side.

Metropolis: the city where Clark Kent (Superman) lives.

S.T.A.R. Labs: a research center in Metropolis, where scientists make high-tech tools and devices for Superman and other heroes.

VISUAL QUESTIONS & PROMPTS

1. In this panel, Livewire uses the word "power" in two ways at once. What are the two ways that "power" can be interpreted in this panel? Explain your answer.

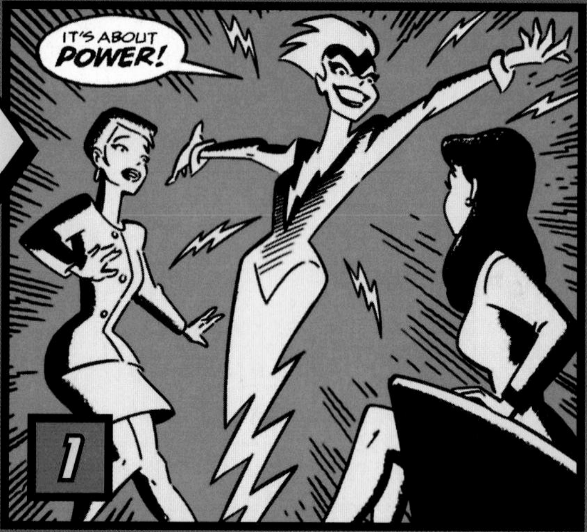

IT'S ABOUT POWER!
1

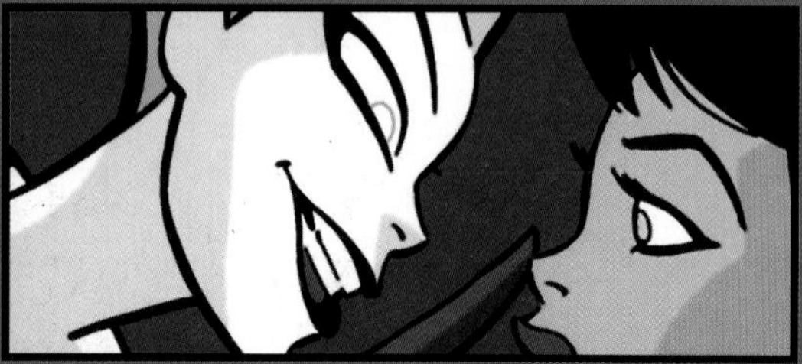

2. In this panel, Livewire is reacting to what is being said in the speech bubbles. How do you think she feels in this panel? Why?

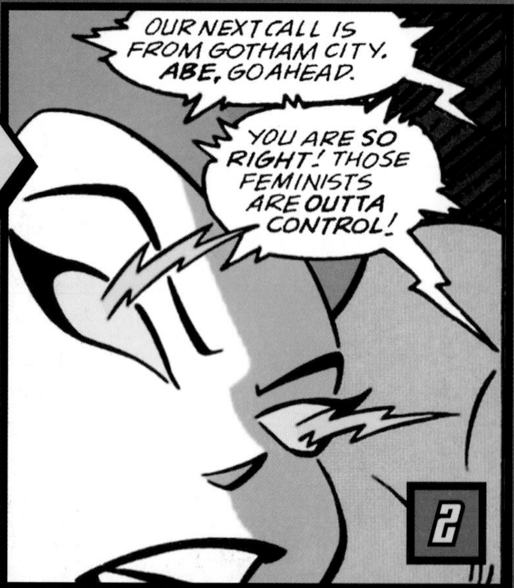

OUR NEXT CALL IS FROM GOTHAM CITY. ABE, GO AHEAD.
YOU ARE SO RIGHT! THOSE FEMINISTS ARE OUTTA CONTROL!
2

3. Why do you think Mercy Graves turned back to look at Livewire and Superman? What do you think she's feeling and thinking? Explain your answers.

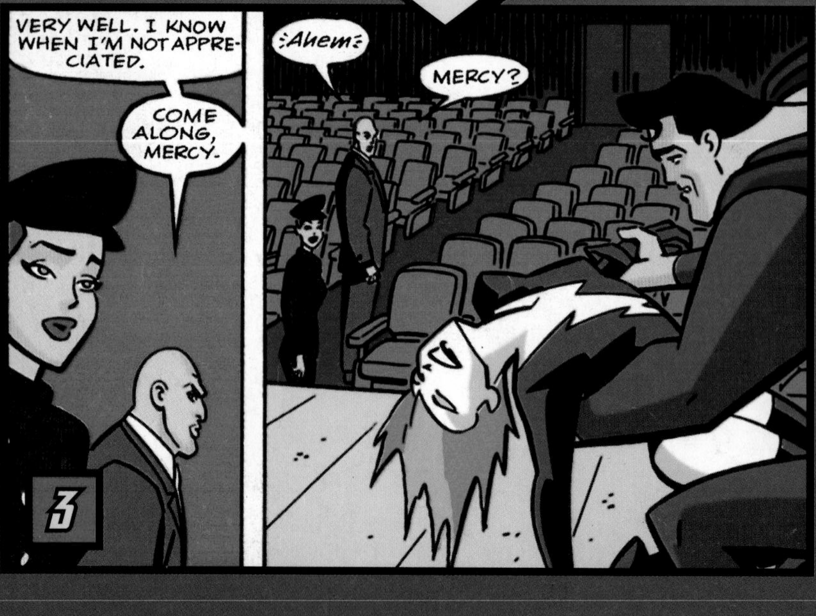

VERY WELL. I KNOW WHEN I'M NOT APPRECIATED.
COME ALONG, MERCY.
3
:Ahem:
MERCY?

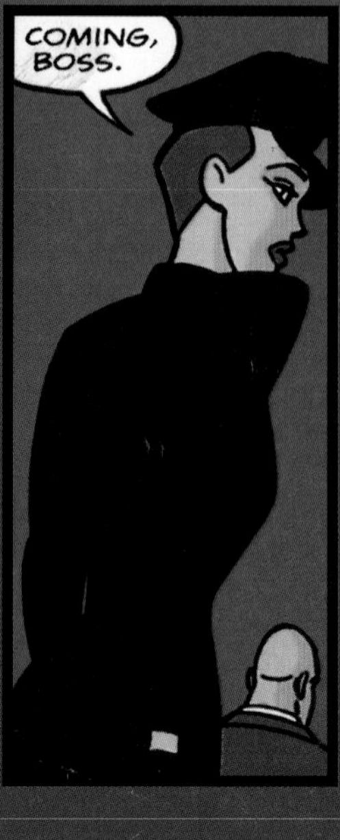

COMING, BOSS.

4. In this panel, we see an outline of Livewire. Using details, describe what you think has just happened in this panel.

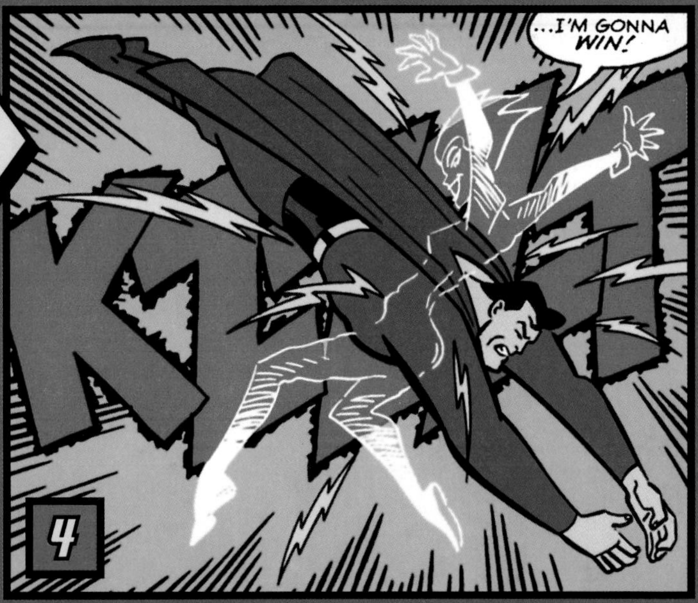

...I'M GONNA WIN!
4

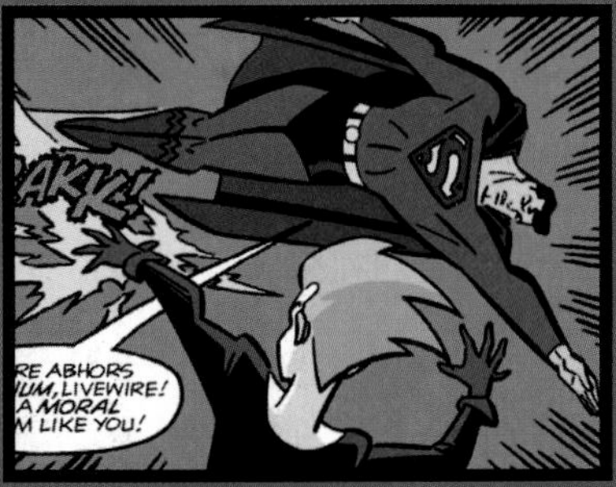

LIVEWIRE!
A MORAL
LIKE YOU!

5. Livewire's hands are blurred in this panel. Why do you think the creators of this comic decided to show her this way?

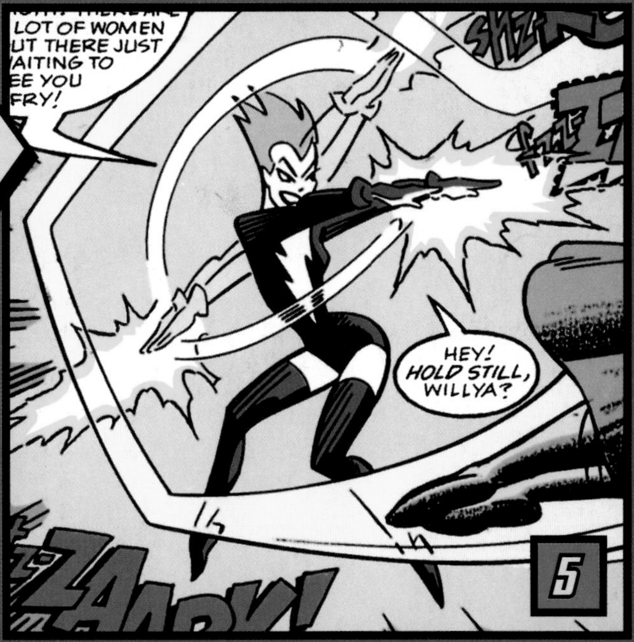

LOT OF WOMEN
FRY!
HEY! HOLD STILL, WILLYA?
5

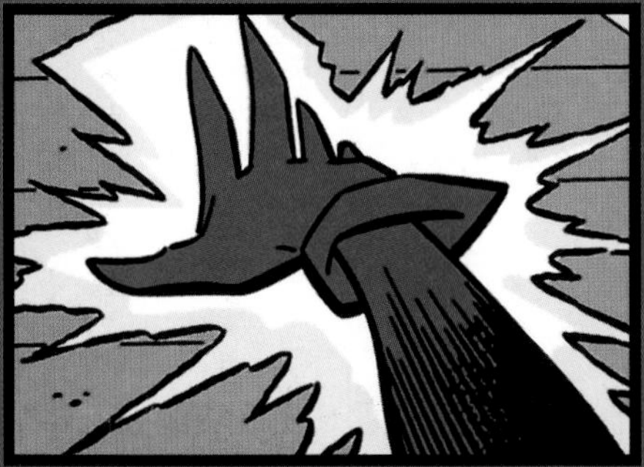

6. At the end of this comic book, this is Superman's expression. How do you think he feels about the outcome of the events? Why?

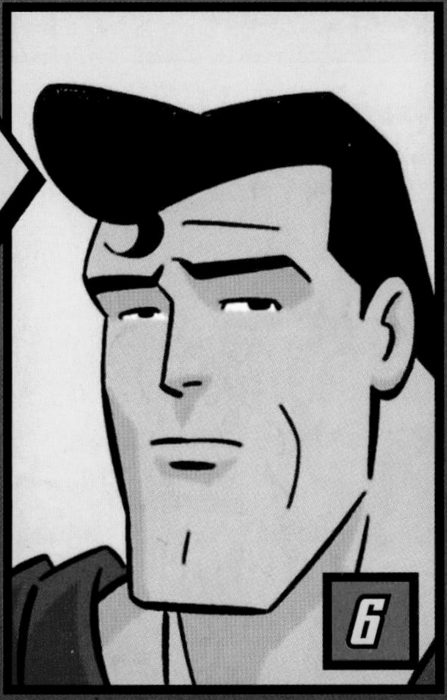

6

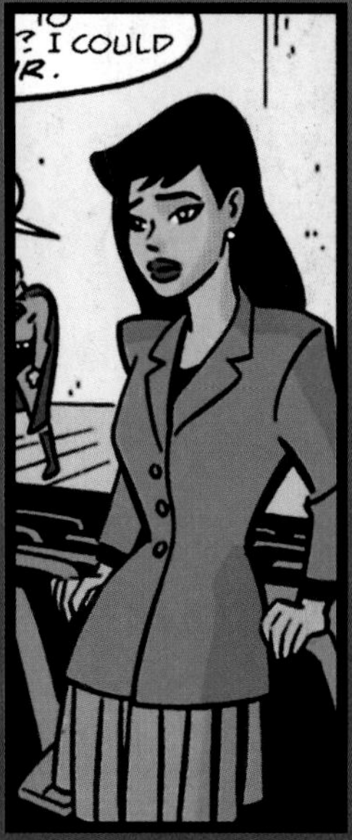

I COULD

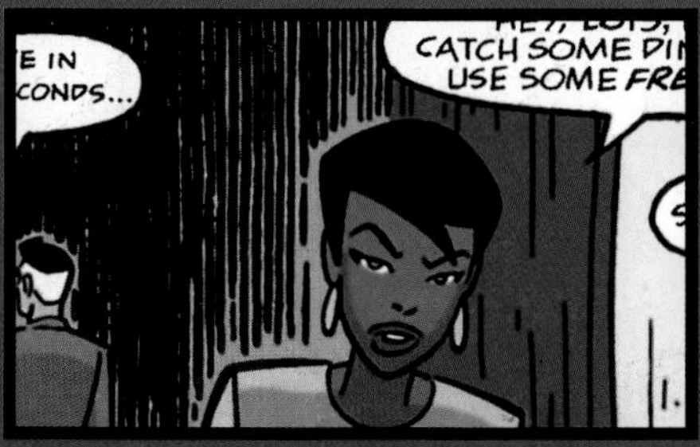

CATCH SOME
USE SOME

SUPERMAN ADVENTURES

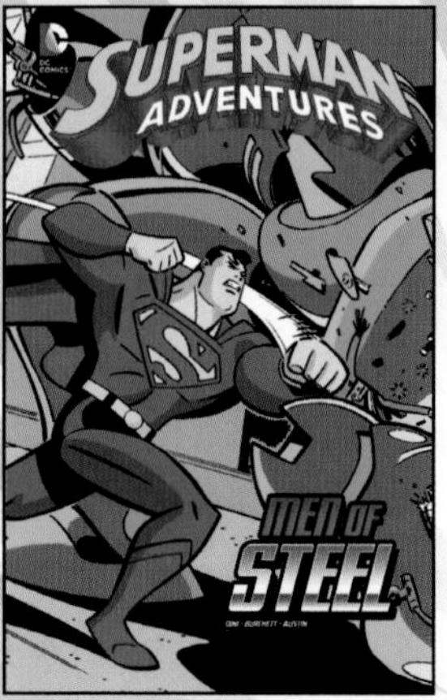
SUPERMAN ADVENTURES
MEN OF STEEL

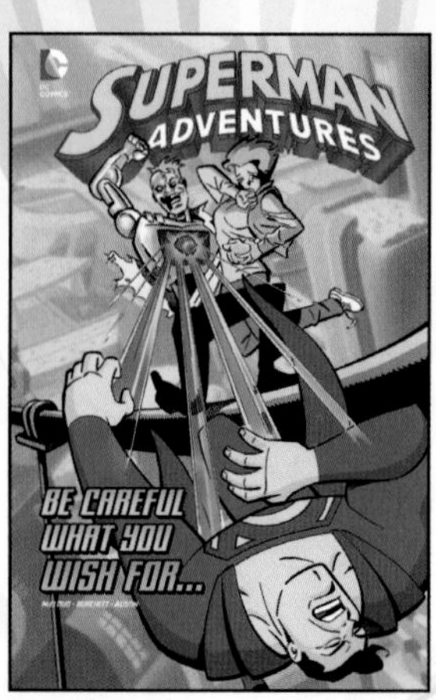
SUPERMAN ADVENTURES
BE CAREFUL WHAT YOU WISH FOR...

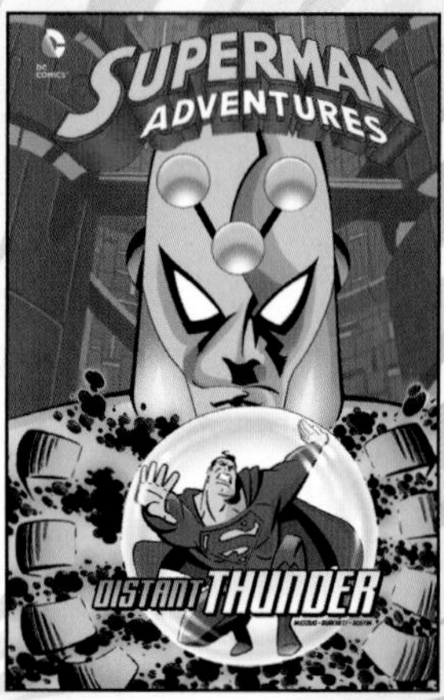
SUPERMAN ADVENTURES
DISTANT THUNDER

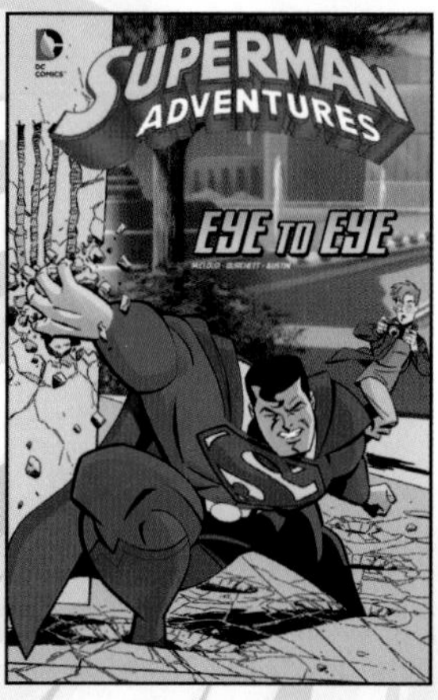
SUPERMAN ADVENTURES
EYE TO EYE

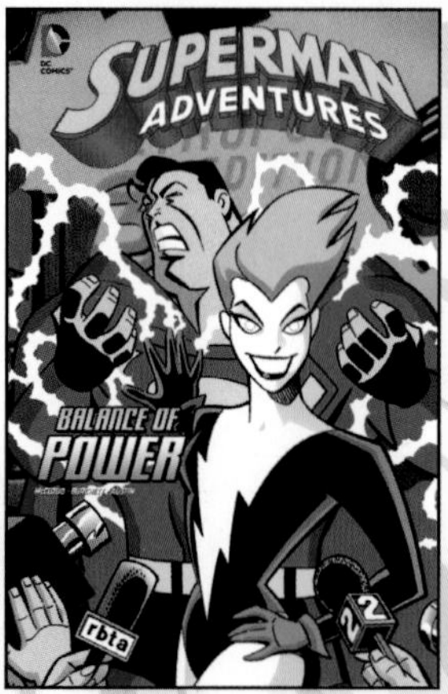
SUPERMAN ADVENTURES
BALANCE OF POWER

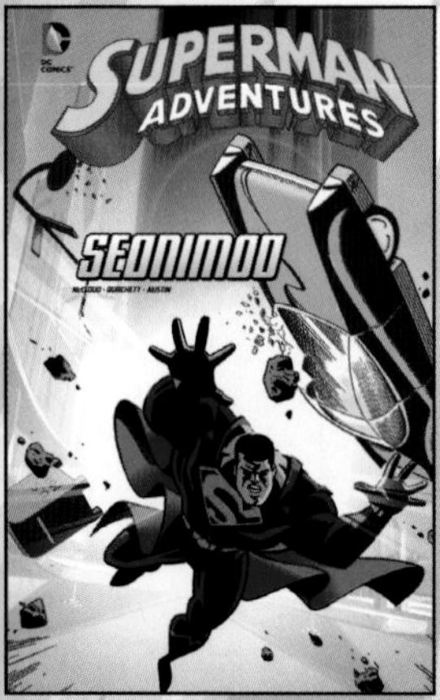
SUPERMAN ADVENTURES
SEONIMOD

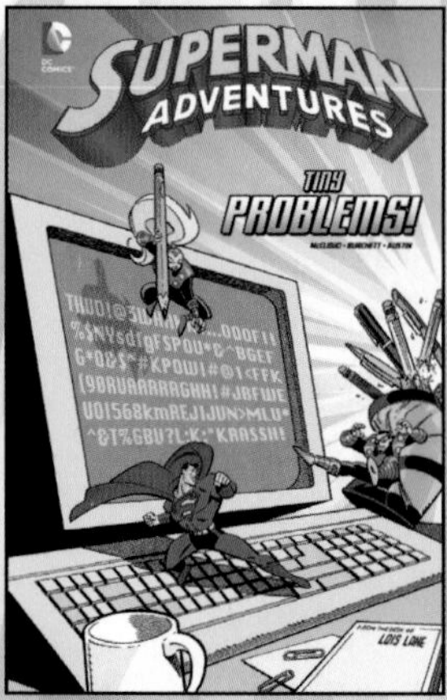
SUPERMAN ADVENTURES
TINY PROBLEMS!

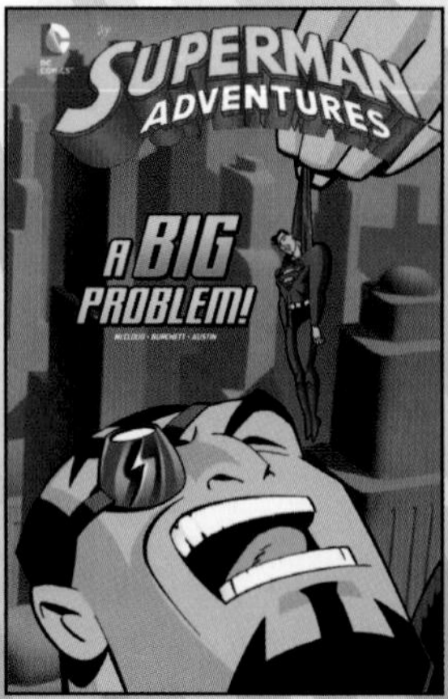
SUPERMAN ADVENTURES
A BIG PROBLEM!